Screams of your Soul

Twelve stories on the aftermath of ignored intuition.

Charletta Green

Copyright © Charletta Green

This is a work of fiction. Environments and exchanges have been rearranged to suit the convenience of the book, and any resemblance to persons living or dead is coincidental. The stories expressed are those of the characters and should not be confused with the author's. The soul lessons are the authors who has so graciously shared them through creative story telling.

ISBN-13979-8-9853939-0-3

For information about custom editions, special sales, premium and bulk purchases, please contact:
Rackhouse Publishing
Rackhousepublishing@mail.com

First Edition

Printed in the U.S.A

Dedication

This book is dedicated to all of us willing to laugh at our most vulnerable moments. Those moments that pulled on our soul, making us want to scream.
Those moments that caused our wings to develop immaturely because we ignored our intuition, our soul's cry.
This read is dedicated to all those caterpillars still crawling to reach their metamorphosis, their liquified moment in life, where life gives you that push and it feels like your soul is being torn from its comfortable place, it is…it's time to leave the comfort of being a caterpillar, staying low to the ground, trying to keep the peace, wanting to get along by muting your voice. Accepting how folks think you should be treated because they think they know what's best for you, when in actuality, they use you for what's best for them.
Here's to those of us feeling our wings develop.
Our SOUL SCREAMS
Realizing it's no longer a "something told me" but it's our intuition directing us to our cocoon, where our wings await us.
After all.
The caterpillar knew it was worth the crawl.

Contents

Acknowledgments

I acknowledge the fact that I enjoyed writing this book. I acknowledge the fact that I had no idea what I was doing. I acknowledge those that encouraged me to write the stories I shared, the lives I post, the advice I gave. I acknowledge my ears for hearing unbelievable things and my memory for retaining those things, making it possible for me to create the characters in these chapters and the stories created around the characters. I acknowledge the fact that I'm exceedingly, abundantly and above the fear that once held me in prison and made me think that I didn't have anything worth writing about.

Charletta "Charlie" Green
@mbellishbycharmega
@screamsofyoursoul

I'm so excited that you've made a decision to read my bestseller, *Screams of Your Soul.* This is a FICTIONAL read, every story is ripped from my imagination. I hope you find the stories as entertaining to read as I found it a joy, (a hilarious joy) to write. Those who know me personally will catch a few fictional realities, so you may just laugh or shake your head and keep reading.

What I want you to take from this book is this:

We can damage ourselves by ignoring our voice, not our vocal cords or the microphone we use for communication. I'm talking about the one we ignore when it's trying to communicate with us, our quiet voice, the one no one hears but you, those conversations our souls have with us, our REAL US, the God in us. That "something told me" or "I knew I should have or shouldn't have" voice. Yeah, good 'ole intuition. I've ignored that voice too many times to count but I can recall situations where it was very clear that my soul was screaming NOOOOOO, and I totally ignored the warning, the guidance that it was screaming at me.

We've dated, married and divorced the wrong people ignoring that voice.

We've become friends with the wrong people, remained friends with the wrong people and lost good friends hanging with the wrong people, ignoring that voice.

We've allowed folks to use us, walk over us, dismiss us… ignoring that voice.

We've deceived ourselves into thinking blood is thicker than common sense, ignoring that scream, that voice.

May these fictional stories entertain you and educate you, may the Soul Lessons give you something to highlight or write on a sticky note to recall later.

Now, let's get into this good read.

1

Innergy

A lesson on identifying love and respecting your intuition .

"Here you go with dat shit!'

A lie, don't care who tells it, this negro just lied! Innergy thinks to herself when her favorite funny guy enters the room. Even comedians must lie to protect their truth. But they'll make a joke about it for the comedic effect, which usually serves them well.

The line up from the comedy show hears the noise coming from the room Innergy is in, and they come inside to see what all the noise is about. The room gets excited, and Innergy is excited because she's meeting the morning show guy. She was on her first "couples date night" with a guy friend named LossVegas, his crew and their wives...everyone is married except for Innergy and Loss Vegas. She's the only girlfriend in the room so she's new to all of the mixed energy she feels in the room...Innergy is nervous but calm. She was blessed with good energy, she was a good vibe but she was unaware of her gift during this season in her life. That's what captured Loss Vegas' attention, he was unaware of how powerful Innergy's energy was. In the room, she felt all eyes and attention on her. The group was used to Loss Vegas being solo, so to see him with a date was rare. They're all having drinks after the show when the line up from the comedy show joins them.

Innergy starts a conversation with the line up...

"I've seen you live before," Innergy says

"The theater, you were on tour with Williams..."

The headliner gets wide eyed and lies to Innergy, "Wasn't

me," he says with his head down, while chewing on the drumette, unable to look Innergy in the eyes. He knew she recognized him, she could tell.

His show opening guy, you know, the guy that preps the crowd for the big act, looks over and gives this look. "What?"

With a bold lie, the comedian looks him up and down and says, "Nope, wasn't me."

Innergy appears puzzled because her memory is on an elephant's level, and she rarely forgot a detail like this one. "Yeah, it was you, I had front row tickets and you talked about the D.C. Sniper. You were running across the stage, you were hilarious, it was you…I saw you," she says with excitement, and so very sure of herself.

The room is full, and she feels like the couples are embarrassed for her because of the information she'd shared about the comedian. He shot it down, and she knew she couldn't debate this guy about his gigs, couldn't call him out as a liar. Especially if he was trying to forget that particular event, I guess he told 'ole dude this was his first time in the city.

Apparently Innergy had called him out on his lie and he had to hold down whatever he'd told his opening act.

But he was funny running across that stage like he was dodging the DC Sniper.

It's important to begin Innergy's story with this information, as it would be a moment to peep into the window of her new relationship, her uninvited opportunity to see the soul nature of the person she was on a date with. It would be Innergy's moment of her truth. Her thoughts, the soul work that needed to be addressed. Little did the comedian know he'd open up a conversation door about Loss Vegas, also known as L.V., and his future plans for his girl Innergy.

"Who's all married here?" the lying comedian would ask…

"All of us, except for this couple here," one of the guys would volunteer. Innergy was cool with the shared information because it was true, and what disturbed her was the response from Loss Vegas…

"Here he goes with that shit!"…her date, Loss Vegas would say aloud…

Loss Vegas was lost in his way with the women in his life and couldn't seem to get it together when it came to dating and enjoying the moments. He had so many loose strings, that's what he would call his many lady friends he'd find himself involved with, and he added Innergy without her permission. He'd given her a part in his play, an unwritten script she'd find herself cast to as one of his characters. He would always take those moments personally and say, "Here he goes with that shit…" That's what he'd say to those married questions moments because he had no intentions on ever being married, and Innergy starts taking those outbursts personally. She sees marriage in her future and isn't trying to be his intermission during his play.

The night went on and the married couples would do their best to make Innergy feel comfortable, Loss Vegas and Innergy were the only ones dating, everyone else was on a husband and wife date night. See, they'd just started their little "romance," they were cute together and comfortable with where they were in their relationship. No pressure, no conversations about commitment, just enjoying the company they would find themselves keeping, often. They were good with what they had, it was fresh. But there was this bug in the room, one that would always bring up marriage and commitment. You know, the bug that always invites discomfort into the room, and it made it very uneasy for LossVegas… "Here you go with that shit," he would say.

Already feeling out of place because of the lie shared by the comedian, Innergy feels she has to defend herself and let it be known she isn't looking to get married…but her soul screams internally, quietly! Thinking to herself, M*arriage is important to me though.* Just share your truth, ask the question, it's already out there. …"What's your beef with marriage?" she asks him.

She defends her honor because she can't believe her date is folding like a lawn chair, running from a question that wasn't even asked. It was just the truth voluntarily given. Innergy shares with the room, "I don't have an issue with marriage, my issue is with the ones that marry but never commit to their mate, the only thing beautiful and glamorous about most of these unions are the wedding pictures full of lies, that's if they had a wedding and the only thing sparkling in most of these unions is the ring, if they wear one…."

One of the wives whispers to another, "What did she say?."

Innergy talks from a familiar place, her scarred place, the soul battle wounds she carries from her past marriage.

The comedians make a joke to try to lift the tension that has overwhelmed the room…although it is filled with tension now, because the laid back girlfriend, Innergy, introduces who she really is by expressing herself…

"I don't need anybody to take care of me and I sure as hell ain't looking to be with somebody with commitment issues. We're dating, that is it," Innergy goes on to say.

Deep down though, Innergy is insulted and embarrassed yet again by her date. Because this isn't her first rodeo with Loss Vegas concerning the topic of marriage. It always finds its way in the marriage conversation when they're together and in the company of a certain nosy body, one of L.V. 's partners in crime.

When they leave the show, once they're alone, she lets him have it. She has a lot of healing to do and her words will cut you if you ever find yourself caught up in her crossfire…that's who Innergy is, a tiny vessel with a lot of fuel to burn. She'd ignite any individual that would test her, not with physical violence, but words that carried a powerful punch. She was strong on image so she'd explode when she felt her image was being attacked, which was twice in one evening and not even two hours apart.

Poor Loss Vegas, he didn't know what hit him… Innergy did. Her mouth explodes, and the words are demeaning and cruel but it's the beginning of what L.V. needs to have a better understanding of who Innergy is. To see her soul and how delicate it is.

The night ends on a sour note, and Innergy knows right then and there that this isn't the guy for her, but she continues to see him because she's so "committed" to the relationship. Loss Vegas displays his "learn to show interest and attention even when you're not into them" skills…you know, show just enough attention to the selected one because it's obvious she's a keeper and you always want to string the keeper along. L.V. knows he isn't ready for a woman like Innergy.

Innergy knows she's too much of a settled woman for L.V., but she stays and commits herself to him for the next two years.

They grew closer and spend quality time together, so he feels comfortable and relaxed. He knows he has her for a long term girlfriend, she's comfortable as well. But he becomes more sloppy with how he treats her, and assumes he has her locked in. He assumes Innergy is satisfied with the time he's willing to spend with her, he assumes he could continue to slip and slide, peep and hide. Loss Vegas assumes himself right into a complete ass…he will simply do what is necessary because it makes him comfortable with being who he really is with the boys. Sneaky, flirty and loose when they'd come together. Eventually, Innergy grows tired of the unanswered calls, no replies or texts and the hidden 'hangout spots....

"You know, we can chill at this spot (house) but I don't want you to know about this spot(honeycomb hideout spot)…Yeah, those spots where you can have a tailgate wife, a cookout girlfriend…you know, where you can be your free self. One of the boys." Those spots where he should've made his selection from when he wanted to "settle down." All those that he'd played with, laid with and stayed with, that's where Loss Vegas should've kept his pole dangling. But he wanted the challenge, the one he had to run after. He didn't want the thirsty, he wanted the thirst quencher, Innergy. She was cool with him wanting what he wanted but her interest and desires for a relationship was different, not difficult, just different and she knew her like-minded mate was out there, and it wasn't him. But he wasn't willing to see it that way. He was sure of himself, and he didn't even see Innergy making her exit.

L.V was losing her, and yet he was clueless about it.

When Innergy realized two years and some days had gone by, she knew it was time to have the talk....

THE CONVERSATION:

Innergy: "Listen, what are we doing here?" What are you doing with those loose strings?"

She asks him because it's obvious there is something holding him back.

Innergy: "What do we have?"

L.V: "We're good, let's not ruin this, why would you ruin this with marriage…I don't ever want to get married."

Innergy: "Well, you won't date me to death, I want to be married, I'm good with being your friend, not your forever girlfriend…no benefits in that…."

L.V: "I'm sorry Innergy, I don't ever want to be married…….we're good with what we got."

Innergy: "No, you're good. I won't have to convince the one that sees my worth that I deserve more, that I'm worth marriage. It's clear you don't think you're worthy of me, so I'll help you with your loose strings and cut myself off."

HER SOUL SCREAMS INSIDE.

He just sits there smirking, because he's certain this will pass and Innergy is just having a moment.

Innergy: "Well, thank you for being so honest, I love and respect you for that, but I love and respect myself more, and I'm not settling for less than what I need, desire or deserve."

With tears in her eyes and strength in her step, she walks away from Vegas.

Innergy would leave the room broken but free. She overstands temporary pain is necessary pain, it's the pain that builds you, teaches you and molds you…so you must allow it, feel it and deal with it. Don't suppress it or your soul will never heal.

That is a difficult breakup for Innergy, as she had poured herself into this relationship, and they were good together. Here's the thing, she was on all the trips, she was the only one with access to his home, vehicles, the couple's club, most events…she had "free range" so she was comfortable, but she wasn't blind, especially when he finally took her to the honeycomb hideout., the spot she'd find out about after she broke up with him. The house where the coochie popper popped up at… Oh, he pulled out all the money from up under all of his mattresses. He was coming clean with Innergy because he wanted her back. It appeared he was hiding nothing.

Immediately realizing his loss, it hit him like darkness. He went on a mission to win Innergy back, he tied all the loose strings, so it appeared, and showed his poker face, or so she thought.

Loss Vegas decided to take Innergy around the crew he was keeping her separated from during their dating time, she thought for sure she'd met everyone that was important to him, but apparently not. It was obvious to Innergy why he didn't want her to be introduced to this crew….yet. With a smile and looking like the mice that got away with the cheese, he introduces her to all the individuals she'd never met, even the one that popped her coochie at him that one time at a party. Innergy noticed how coochie popper was shocked and hurt that Loss Vegas had a plus one with him this time. Innergy picked up on the sexual tension coochie popper was giving off. The questions she'd answer about Loss Vegas let Innergy know she knew him, and that he was catching her coochie and could still get it…that's why he'd never bothered to bring her to this place. Innergy peeped how much coochie popper knew about her man but kept her cool. She doesn't entertain thirsty.

See, here's the story about coochie popper:

She was at a party where L.V and Innergy popped in, and she spots L.V, smiles and pops her coochie at him. She starts dancing her way over to him, and even though L.V. swipes her away and turns his back to her, letting her know he isn't alone, she stops, leans back and gives a look at Loss Vegas, like, 'What the fuck! Oh, it's like dat nigga?' and she dances the night away, alone.

'So, we meet again, Coochie Popper,' Innergy thinks to herself when she enters this new clubhouse belonging to Loss Vegas's boys.

So, this is that house... This explains a lot, especially that cold shoulder she once received from one of the individuals she'd run into again at The Honeycomb Hideout…Cold shoulder and Coochie Popper were girls, and Cold Shoulder was always invited to Loss Vegas's events so, Innergy knew Cold Shoulder and it was clear why she gave Innergy that bad energy when they first met. Cold Shoulder was aware Loss Vegas was playing her girl. Listen, folks will get "their tail" in a wagging mess, won't they?

Innergy watches, listens and questions herself, "Why am I just being introduced to this group of people?" It's apparent to Innergy that L.V spends a lot of time with this group…and Miss Coochie Popper….

L.V. and Innergy were going on over two years of dating and Innergy couldn't accept the fact she was just meeting this group and coming to this house, it was obvious Loss Vegas spent quality time with these people, this was family. She had every reason to be puzzled by this encounter of the new friend's kind. It was at that moment, Innergy knew to protect herself and remove Loss Vegas completely from her life. She wouldn't though, she'd stay and play her part, Loss Vegas had officially cast her as Lead Loose String. She would sit there hurt and insulted. It was like meeting the parents after the wedding….

She knew this wasn't a place, a position she desired, but he wanted what he thought he lost, the one that "got away…." It would become obvious to Innergy that wanting her back and putting in all the effort to win her back was just another part of Loss Vegas's Screen Play.

There were so many that desired Loss Vegas, and they'd make sure to show their thirst for him, especially when he'd bring Innergy around. He was becoming very comfortable parading their "committed" relationship around in front of those that couldn't understand why Loss Vegas selected Innergy and not them. They'd say all kind of ignorant outbursts when Vegas would bring Innergy around:

*Vegas was looking at my momma's booty.

*Let's talk about cheaters.

*Is Innergy with him?

There were a few of them who would be bothered when Innergy was present. That was an "in your face" indication that Loss Vegas would play with these mice when the cat wasn't with him.

They were thirsty and would say or do anything to try to create tension in the room, to make Innergy uncomfortable, and plant seeds of mischievousness.

Just thirsty and mad at Innergy for "taking away" their quencher.

It would be these moments that Innergy's soul would scream. *"RESCUE US FROM THIS, YOU SEE WHAT THIS IS. DON'T TAKE THE PART, LET THEM HAVE VEGAS, YOU NEVER AUDITIONED FOR THIS, GIVE HIM HIS SCRIPT BACK......WE DESERVE TO BE SOMEONE'S LEADING ROLE, NOT A STANDBY."*

Innergy ignored the screams of her soul and became a part of the cast, his leading lady. It appeared she was his only soul desire, his soulmate but his soul was restless and Innergy had a way about her that calmed his singleness anxiety. She would regret ignoring her soul's cry. She would constantly find herself hating Loss Vegas because of the decision she made, and decided to deceive her truth to live in his pleasure. She knew he wasn't ready for what she had to offer, the commitment, stability and calm, but she would take all her pearls and cast them to his swine ways.

14

Never settle once you see it for what it really is. Sometimes, seeing comes immediately and we'll write it off as the individual having a bad day or moment. When it becomes bad days and constant moments, LISTEN TO YOUR SOUL. Stop listening with your feelings and emotions and the years connected to the situation. Listen to that QUIET SCREAM OF YOUR SOUL. It's what so many of us call our gut feeling. If you ignore your soul, at least listen with your eyes, believe what they're showing you more than what they're saying. Actions speak loud!. A person means just what they're saying through their ACTIONS. Just like the Bible says, "The heart is deceitful above all things and desperately wicked, who can know it." Ain't that the truth!

Don't follow your heart, listen to your soul.

2
Boldlicious

A lesson in how to recognize snakes in your bushes

"What is it about her? Is it that bald head? I'm just trying to figure this thing out…"

This is the conversation taking place right in front of Boldlicious, concerning her.

"Just look at her," the gentleman replies. "she's inviting, she's pleasant, her smile is beautiful," he continues.

The obviously jealous 'friend' looks away in disgust, that's not the answer Friendneva was looking for, especially after pointing out Boldlicious' bald head.

Boldlicious is a bold soul. Full of laughter and life and care, you know…that friend. So secure in herself that she knows she is the friend. She's not the made up kind, you know, make up, push up clothes and purchased hair. She's definitely a what you see is what you get, no peeling away layers in a bedroom setting type of woman.

It didn't matter to her that Friendneva was jealous of her, that was Neva's problem, not Bold's problem. Bold once loved the relationship she shared with Neva….Neva was that 'friend.' She was crazy fun and held great conversations, and she was kind, but it came with a price: she wanted you to love what she loved and hate what she hated. People, places and things. Boldlicious was her challenge, so she admired and welcomed the opposite attracts friction.

Years would pass and the two would remain the best of associates, I'll use associates because Boldlicious was clueless about her 'friend', Friendneva being the type of friend she was….actually, Bold considered them sister friends.

The relationship was seasoned and 'secured.' That's what Bold thought.

Now, let's get into the knitty gritty of this Frenemy (an enemy disguised as a friend) relationship…

Boldlicious had a boyfriend that turned into a fiancé, that never turned into a husband…

We'll talk about BakedBean later, that's an entire chapter of its own.

After a year of dating, BakedBean proposed to Boldlicious, and she said yes. He was a great guy *and* a whore. Yes, that's possible. Bold was good for BakedBean, she helped him with his seed situation (Poppa was a rolling stone, like his sister said, he'd fuck it if it had a hole…) Like I said, his chapter is coming…

Well, Friendneva had invited herself to Bold's boo, BakedBean… and he didn't turn it down.   Knowing him, he turned it on and up. Your nature is your nature and their nature was high, and neither one of them were Scorpio's…. Y'all know what they say about a Scorpio. Anyway, those two Zodiacs ended up sharing nature together.

Boldlicious was aware of this but needed to hold onto BakedBean just a little while longer because, "Cash rules everything around her," and he was kind with his cash.

Listen, we'll get to BakedBean but he must be shared in this story as well. Neva never knew that Bold knew what she knew so she was comfortable with Bold, that's what Boldlicious was, a Friend that could keep a secret. People trusted her and there was something inviting about her that would have folks spilling their deepest secrets. Neva secrets and nature ran deep…Streets will put your shoes on and your business out there.

There was something about Boldlicious that Friendneva couldn't shake, and that was her kindness. Love and kindness is a magnet, its power is pulling. Bold was a magnet.

Friendneva didn't want the baldhead that Boldlicious sported, she wanted the attention, the love, the beauty and the men. Boldlicious could attract by simply being her bald-headed self. The bald and the beauty….

Boldlicious moved on from BakedBean and was free and loving. Neva was still clueless that Bold knew about her role in the sheets with BakedBean.

Let's move on.

Months later, Bold would meet WhyMe. WhyMe was handsome, fun and 'stable,' but he was stuck in his past. His ex still had him by the balls but without the sex. He was holding on to her ghost, she was very much alive but he was dead to her. WhyMe still had pictures of her, and jewelry that belonged to her. He was still hanging tight with her family, although she wasn't, as she was doing her own thing with someone else's married thing. It really is what it is.

WhyMe finally moved on once he met Boldlicious. She was good for him, she helped him to discover his why.

WhyMe had a friend that wasn't a friend but he didn't care, he just loved having 'friends.' Well, WhyMe's friend, Kneepolean, was a backdoor kind of guy. He got wind that Boldlicious and Friendneva were friends, and thought they too were friend friends. See, Neva's friends came with benefits, and didn't mind bending over and giving it away. Being that KNEEpolean and Friendneva were FuckFriends, and with Neva nature being so high, surely Boldlicious was the same bird, since she flocked with Friendneva. Did I mention that KNEEpolean and WhyMe were boys, partners, mancave brothers.

'I DON'T KNOW WHAT IT IS ABOUT THAT BALD HEAD….'

Knee wanted him some Bold, by any means necessary. He didn't care who Bold was dating. He asked Friendneva to set up the stage, she prepared the hookup, she was all in.

Knowing Bold is now dating WhyMe did not trouble Neva's soul because she got off on this kind of foolery.

The conversation:

Knee: Go and hook that up for me, Neva…

(Neva calls Bold to one side.)

Neva: Me and Knee used to fuck, his dick bigger than this remote in my hand…

(Bold isn't moved with her example of the size of KNEE's

hang.) WhyMe is in the next room, and Bold is trying to piece this thing together. "Why are we discussing this man and y'all past, and his hang?"

Boldlicious: (Very dry.) Wow…

Friendneva: Yeah, I was hooked on that thang.

(Bold just stares.)

Now it's awkward because Boldlicious isn't biting. The two rejoin the party, and Bold is angry and ready to go. WhyMe and Bold leave…after Bold sees WhyMe licking his tongue out at Neva. Yeah, you read that correctly. Bold catches WhyMe pulling his seat in to get a good look at Neva's pie and offers his tongue to lick her crust. Bold just sits there and looks at him with disgust and WhyMe sees her, and the shame on his face says it all.

The next day, WhyMe is sober enough for Bold to share last night's events. WhyMe is angry and troubled about the penis offer, so it seems, but not to the point of removing himself from the friend list of Kneepolean, after all, Bold did catch WhyMe licking out his tongue at Friendneva while looking between her legs. So, maybe Knee and WhyMe had already discussed pie swapping, not knowing that Bold's Pie wasn't Community Pie.

Bold overstands why eagles fly alone and nest high.

Buzzards…

Realizing she's hanging with buzzards, Boldicious drops Neva from her friend list permanently. Boldlicious is no longer drunk on trying to figure out Neva's motives or trying to remain friends with someone that obviously wanted to introduce Bold to a swinging way of life.

Bold was disturbed that Neva saw her as that girl, instead of putting Knee in his place and telling him, "She's NOT that girl!" You can try her but I've known her long enough to know she's not like me.

Don't get it twisted, Bold did her thing but it was her thing to do and her decision on who she'd do it with.

WhyMe should've been removed that evening as well but she would give him a pass….while her soul screamed, 'FOUL! GET RID OF HIM NOW!'!

Boldlicious never took Knee up on his offer by way of her 'friend' Neva, but she was always alarmed that WhyMe was cool with remaining boys with this back door Santa…

He explained that it may have been Friendneva's idea so why trouble the waters. WhyMe knew of Neva's ways and deeds, several of his friends knew of Neva's sexual appetite, so, it made sense to him because of how the boys talked about Neva.

Her soul screams: WHY IS IT SO DIFFICULT FOR YOU TO SEE THAT THIS NEGRO AIN'T YO FRIEND! WAKE DA HELL UP! THIS NIGGA SET UP THE ENTIRE EVENING TO MAKE A PUSSY APPOINTMENT WITH YOUR GIRL. AND YOU COOL WITH THAT! WHAT HAVE I SIGNED UP FOR? Her soul screams. DID Y'ALL PLAN THIS, IS THIS HOW YOU ACTUALLY GET DOWN,

YOU WANT YOU SOME NEVA LIKE THE REST OF' EM? WHY HAS ALL OF THIS INVITED ITSELF INTO MY LIFE? I DON'T DISPLAY THIS TYPE OF BEHAVIOR. WE AIN'T COOL WITH THIS. Bold hears the scream and ignores her soul's warning.

Bold continues to date WhyMe, she's certain of his potential but clueless to his addiction to strange fruits. Knee needs WhyMe's friendship because he's determined to get his hands on Boldlicious, and even if he can't bed her, he's cool with a cheap feel or sexual conversation in the company of Bold. Anything to get his penis high off, his secret lust for Boldlicious.

Bold knew there was some type of secrecy between the two friends because what man would be comfortable with another man constantly trying his girl? As long as Knee knew his place, Bold was good with being in his company but it was disturbing to Bold how comfortable WhyMe was with having this lust maggot around his girl.

Some time later, Knee would try his feel one mo gen with Boldlicious. He sees her, he notices that WhyMe's back is turned, Knee grabs Bold and hugs her. He steps back to look at her and then, without hesitation, slaps her on her wide hips and says, "Boldlicious!!"

She's not shocked because she knows this snake very well, and has been dealing with his slithering ways for several years now, but she knows in her soul that this is his last sexual attempt, his last invite. She steps back and catches the wicked stare from Knee, as if he was saying to her, "I can have you anytime I want to and WhyMe punk ass can't do nut'n about it…."

She gives a unexpected reply to his sexual harassment…

"You're real special…"

And she walks off.

She listens to her soul scream, the advice her soul shares in that moment:

Give him nothing! He's not worth your emotion, leave him begging for more.

For the first time, in the presence of Kneepolian, Boldlicious displays her boldness. In this moment, silence is actually golden.

Because she left him empty, emotionless, he wanted more. Boldlicious took her seat next to her clueless man, WhyMe. He finally turns to give her some attention:

The scene: sitting at the bar….

WhyMe: You want something to drink?

Boldlicious: Yes.

They order the drinks.

Knee squeezes his body between WhyMe and Boldlicious….

Knee: Whatcha drinking, Boldlicious?

Bold: Remy and Spite. (Her uncle's favorite cocktail.)

The drinks are ordered, and Bold sips and places her drink down..

Knee reaches for her drink, she's shocked but smooth with it, giving away none of her emotion. Knee sips her drink from her straw and puts it back down on the bar....

Knee: Damn, that's strong!

WhyMe is so deep in his conversation with his boy at the bar that he's clueless to all of the betrayal going on behind his back.

Boldlicious: : Yeah, it's nice.

She picks the drink up and knocks it over.

Knee: Damn Bold, that's a ten dollar drink..

Quietly she starts cleaning up her spillage, and WhyMe finally remembers he's there with Bold, and turns around to see what happened. He offers to purchase another drink, and Boldlicious declines. With WhyMe's attention finally on Bold, Knee slithers his way out from between the two of them.

Boldlicious shares with WhyMe what went down once the evening is over and they're home and doing their Netflix and chill, she leaves out zero details. WhyMe is angry and promises to deal with it:

"You'll never have to worry about Knee ever again,"
WhyMe proclaims.

Promises, promises, Boldlicious thinks to herself.

Bold knew she'd never have to deal with Knee's disrespectful ass ever again. She'd already prepared herself for her next encounter with Knee. She was going to help Knee with his Kneepolian spirit since it was obvious that WhyMe was still dreaming about how many licks it took to get to Neva's center.

People with snake tendencies are dangerous, cunning and vicious. Their words and deeds are venomous to the unprepared and the trusting. They're quick to say, "You misunderstood me, I'd never do anything to hurt you..." They know how to strike you with hurt and deception because that's who they are. They are slick and coiling with their ways. They try to get you in their grip. Once they become comfortable with you, they shed their skin and expose who they really are. Their squeeze becomes tighter, suffocating you, but they've so cunningly manipulated you with their "charm" that you can't feel the poison. These individuals love to get in so close, they love to know personal things about you. The intent is to have something on you to keep you committed to their purpose for their life. You sense their deception and you even question it at times but you go with it. All along your soul is screaming inside of you....SNAKE! Pay attention to these signs, the soul knows. We call it intuition.

3

Somuchsoul

A Lesson To Reveal That Sometimes Age Is Just A Number

"Just give me six months to prove to you that age ain't nothing but a number," he tells SoMuchSoul once she finds out he's ten years her junior.

She remembers watching him perform at the jazz lounge. SoMuchSoul was there at Toot Your Own Horn Jazz Spot when she heard this sultry voice, and it was him again, the dude from the other place, Pour and Stir Monday's, her favorite Monday night spot. She loved that place because it was small, loud and crowded with adults…a break from the kids. Newly divorced and excited about it, SoMuchSoul was out to smoove and groove.

"Coming to the stage," the DJ blares, "give it up for the band JustwhatIneed featuring HeKanSing."

The crowd gathers and the band begins to play. She listens and takes it all in and she leaves. She's a music lover, a mixed media type of listener, so she's satisfied. Later that week, at Toot Your Own Horn, she gets the chance to compliment him on his singing, and HeKanSing responds with a warm and smiling, "Thank you."

That was it for her because she was free and loving herself. Not interested in knowing more about him, she just wanted him to know she's a fan of his performances. Come Sunday, he's the guest choir host, and he sees her and makes sure to spark up a conversation in the parking lot after service. He asks her out on a date.

SoMuchSoul smiles and says, "How old are you?"

He replies, "Thirty."

She laughs and says, "You're too young but thanks, I'm flattered." It was clear he was younger, yet, he carried himself so maturely, and he seemed wise and confident. SoMuchSoul isn't interested at all, until he presents his six-month dating trial. He sells his dating plan and it's interesting, so she gives it a chance, and agrees to his proposal. It's different. After all, what immature man would think to ask for a dating probation? .A slick and sneaky one.

LET THE DATING BEGIN….

It starts out nice and slow, perfect for SoMuchSoul because he isn't trying her, he's just enjoying her, dating her.

Eventually, she bites and it was off and running. Unfortunately, the lust king was sitting on HeKanSing's throne, and those six months ended up being a lesson in growing pains for them both. SoMuchSoul realized she had a lot of growing up to do when it came to controlling her feelings, and her age became just a number. All respect for her ten years senior over HeKanSing was a joke to him. He'd soon realize he could play his distress card because SoMuchSoul was a nurturing soul, it was definitely in her DNA, an empath to her core. She discovered things about him that would make an elderly man blush. She didn't judge him, she supported him, encouraged him to face his 'demons' and clear out his baggage. In other words, stop running. What's done is done and hiding from your purpose will only cause future embarrassment and pain. His deeds were deep but she related because she had her shameful moments. Her closet.

Six months later, things are smoothing out and love actually begins to bloom and she gets it. SoMuchSoul sees HeKanSing relaxed, exposed and free to be seen, which allows more dating time. He begins to address his emotions and shame, things he'd want forever hidden, she'd be the one to coach him into his healing place.

SoMuchSoul knew it was time to get real about this dating game, he had situations that he had no desire to shake, and she allowed him in deep. He knew it, and charmed her. He was far from being good at his game though because boys will be boys and he left the safety of her sandbox to build sand houses with another.

HeKanSing had no idea that SoMuchSoul was grown and knew how to gather her toys and leave the playground when dirt was being thrown, and she'd had enough because she realized this pawn never wanted to be king. He came to a chess game playing checkers, well, not even checkers, tic-tac-toe. He'd begin to do those sneak and seek games, the ones that conveniently would have him on music assignments. But these sets would be the one on one "my body's calling for ya" concerts….

SoMuchSoul had seen enough and invested enough. It was time to cash in on this overrated concert.

He had committed himself to too much booty and it was catching up with him.

Her soul screams: WHY AM I HERE? HOW DID I GET THIS DEEP INTO THIS CASTLE AND END UP IN THIS DUNGEON? I AGREED TO DATE A KNIGHT IN SHINING ARMOR FOR SIX MONTHS, NOT A DRESSED UP PAWN WANTING TO BE A KING. WHY AM I MAKING ALL OF THESE BAD MOVES, PLAYING CHECKERS ON THIS CHESS BOARD? GIRL, TURN THIS BOARD OVER AND GET OUT OF THIS FAIRYTALE. THIS KING IS SITTING ON A SHITTY THRONE.

SoMuchSoul decided to pull the curtains on this overrated concert tour, especially when she found herself being the bailout person for one of his great venue ideas that flopped. SoMuchSoul would love to get those coins back. She discovered all she needed to know to get out of this dating contract with HeKanSing, all the resources had dried up and SoMuchSoul didn't have to create the exit, HeKanSing was talented but stupid and figured he could get over on SoMuchSoul because her kindness appeared as a weakness to him. Her kindness was her calm and she made sure to introduce him to her twin sister, YouTriedIt.

Needless to say, He didn't like when YouTriedIt took over, she's a crafty one. She is the investigator, the cold one, the "don't try me" one. The Hyde to SoMuchSoul's Jekyll. He introduced his coldness and YouTriedIt gave him the chills.

SoMuchSoul really enjoyed what it was, 'while it was'. She had a great time raising that thirty something year old boy, she definitely took him to school. Hopefully HeKanSing thinks about his offers before presenting a verbal dating contract these days…

SoMuchSoul went on to hitting higher notes and her new lover is music to her ears.

Don't upset your life when all is going smooth, when you're in your music moment of life, hearing all the lyrics. Don't allow the flute player to come in and lead you off your path like a mice….recognize noise when it's noise. She still supports his efforts, he'll make sure to grab her attention when he spots her in the audience. She still makes him very giddy, and it's adorable. Her soul whispers, "Look at Momma's man, all grown up."

It's as if he can hear her approval, you can see the blush in his face. He's always certain to acknowledge her when he sings, and SoMuchSoul always catches it. Every now and again, HeKanSing will show his age but he's still a little boy on the inside needing that attention. He gets all nervous when the crowd is full of women, knowing he's had the pleasure of whispering sweet nothings between their legs. Most people won't know you're a fool until you volunteer the information by opening your big mouth, singing all ya business.

Age is just a number, it's not a cougar number, it's not a sugar daddy number…it's just a number celebrated once a year, that's what age is. Age is just a number. You tell your age by the way you handle your situations, your life moments, your conversations, your willingness to let go, your control of self when you wanna let 'em have it. Your absolute power to forgive, your ability to cover and protect. Your way of communicating. We are a society that's quick to say I'm grown and we have so many individuals with a kindergarten mentality, still trying to figure it out. Instead of maturing and developing from our knee scrapes and falls, most of us are still kicking and falling on the floor and having tantrums. I know some individuals well seasoned(aged) and they gossip and create mess like you'd expect a teenager or younger person to do. They never grow up, they never mature, they just age but they never develop, and wisdom never becomes their friend. Muhammad Ali said it best! "A man that views life at fifty the same way he viewed life at 20, has wasted thirty years of his life."

4

Lovelife

A Lesson On Anointed Lust & Identifying Lust Wrapped In Righteousness

"I can't believe this sanctified negro just tried me like that!"

Bishop PleaseHer inboxed LoveLife, inboxing was before you had to have a messenger to receive your messages…

"Happy birthday," he writes.

"Thank you," LoveLife replies.

"How old are you?" he asks.

"Forty,'" she responds.

"So that's forty licks I owe you,"

Bishop PleaseHer would write….

She never responded to his insulting lick invite, and only deletes and blocks him. She overstands the offer and isn't about to help him get his rocks off. She was aware of his history with women so she wasn't interested in becoming the next victim to his lust desires.

LoveLife is her name, playing church ain't her game so she was not about to entertain this pulpit whore.

She'd experienced this ministry before so she wasn't shocked, just angry because it made her question herself. She wondered what it was about her personally, what was she giving off, what energy, what vibe….was it sexually? Why would he reach out to her?

Her soul screamed within: WHAT IN THE HELL? What am I doing to make him think it's cool to come at me crossways? Wanting to reward my pie with forty licks from his tongue! What would his church family and first lady think about this private bible study he's trying to have with me? Why does this three-piece suit wearing "saint" see me as a two-piece snack? What in all levels of Hell? Do they think I'm supposed to be honored by this attention, this lust of the eye from the "ordained"?

This was one of the telling signs that this ministry was in need of a lust and fornicating exorcism. One of the reasons LoveLife left the Old Ways Ministries.

Bishop PleaseHer was spiritually wounded and he knew it, he just cared nothing about it and it filtered its way through his congregation. The praise and worship song should've been, "Where my hoes at?" It was obvious there was a sexual strong hold all up in old ways ministries. The messages would always end up supporting whatever Bishop PleaseHer was dealing with personally or knew about, personally, concerning one of his church members, he would try to "ministerfy," that's to justify why someone was in a "fallen" way when the church knew the business of the one fallen. But wait, those messages were specifically for those big band members, big tithers, rules don't apply if your checkbook could buy your redemption. Especially if you became pregnant, they'd treat it like the hospital, are you insured or uninsured? If you're insured, like being the pastor's daughter or a favorite to the minister or ministry, .or a cash thrower, it would be like welcoming simba, it was natural, it was the circle of life. But the uninsured....baby, you need to go somewhere and sit down, we can't accept your "bastard" birth here but the county will take you.

When he reached out to her, inboxing her, she knew it was for no good, he could've left a happy birthday comment like everyone else. Why would that slut reach out to her once she was gone from their corrupt ministry? He apparently felt like the rumors that her ex was speaking about her were true. Had he known her spirit, he wouldn't have tried her.

Here's the brew, things that happen before you can sip tea. LoveLife had spiritual breaking after spiritual breaking altercation while being a member at Old Ways Ministries. She'd witnessed the deception and not so well-hidden human weaknesses. Before all of the craziness, when everything was covered with sheets, she was excited about her new church and all it had to offer when she visited and eventually decided to become a member.

LoveLife ended up there at Old Ways Ministry after she was "forced" to leave her other church home because her husband kept accusing her of flirting with the pastor's son at this particular church. To keep the peace, she would follow her insecure mate to a church home that was pleasing to him…Old Ways Ministries. One of many church membership disappointments LoveLife would experience before faithfully attending BSM(Bed Side Ministries).

Old Ways appeared to have had a lot to offer, very inviting and there was finally a peace in her short term, attending a church her mate agreed with. He felt comfortable and walked in agreement with everything about the church.

LoveLife would become a part of several ministries and attend often and she became faith family orientated. She started inviting individuals to attend with her, and a few would join. It was beautiful. You'd swear it was "the move of God…"

Even though LoveLife wasn't in love with her mate, she was committed. She knew the marriage wouldn't last long at all. You can't fix the foundation once the concrete begins to settle, you have to be committed to doing the work of destroying the dysfunctional habits and commit to building on truth and honesty. Her union was built on lies and pain and control. The only thing you can do with a foundation like that is break it up. Don't build on it. LoveLife knew this marriage was doomed from the beginning because she married out of pity. She was destructive when she broke the relationship off with this mate, so out of pocket that they gave her mate thirty days to move off of the property LoveLife had caused graffiti damage to. She'd reached her "hate you" level with this person and she reacted to his evil and wicked manipulative ways. She tried to walk away but the mate made it damn near impossible. LoveLife would find herself losing herself, wanting to satisfy her soon to be husband.

Feeling responsible for his circumstance, being "homeless," she agreed to marry him in those thirty days and try to make it work. Yeah, it's still not tea sipping time, this story is still brewing, this insert is necessary so you'll understand her screaming soul, the importance of never ignoring your intuition or your God voice, the God in you when its message is clear and loud.

Well, the ministry knew very little about LoveLife and The Mate's relationship because they joined the ministry looking like a happy couple, well put together (but a walking deception). Shortly after joining and becoming heavily involved with Old Ways Ministry, the couple couldn't pretend any longer. Well, LoveLife couldn't.

She'd reached her salvation moment and was done with The Mate and The Ministry. Shit had hit the altar. LoveLife would experience individuals having affairs and favor given to "tithe payers and big monetary givers" and disrespect for things spiritual, especially that one time the praise dancer popped her coochie in front of her married lover. Sister Soulwhore danced her praise to her side piece, it definitely wasn't to God, it was to the stripper pole, lap dance god, .and that one time that brother came out stepping with his cane on the pulpit because he was just released from prison because he was a thief and was caught, and had to go away for a short bid. Instead of him humbling, returning to the church and having several seats and allowing the hand of God to move on his behalf, he floated in on the favor of Bishop PleaseHer. You can imagine the insult that must've been to so many of the other members that were pulled from their positions for a far lesser church "embarrassment." But, here comes the candy cane stepping Armor Bearer, stepping across the pulpit, giving the congregation a step show, inviting us to kiss his ass because, "Look at God…"

After that performance, LoveLife was done. She begins to plan her 'escape', she'd had enough of the flirting Pastor and the accepting wife of all this foolery, the "born with a silver bible in their mouth children" and 'immoral' human acceptance of what was and wasn't godly in their tunnel vision sight.

She knew it was time to leave when the pastor and his wife called her one night and asked her if she was with one of the brothers from the church because her insecure mate saw her leave with this brother and called them and said he witnessed this. So to give him a peace of mind, they called LoveLife and asked this humiliating question, at one o'clock in the freaking morning. Hours before Sunday service.

"Sister LoveLife, are you with Brother SlangPenis? Your husband is calling and says you're not home, you left with Brother SlangPenis after the service…"

LoveLife was home in her bed, sound asleep, hoping her husband would stay out all night looking for her. She started to stay home that Sunday after this "I'm concerned" phone call but she pressed on. The brother she was accused of being with approached her in the parking lot that morning, and apologized to LoveLife because they'd called him as well. Let's just say he wasn't with LoveLife but he wasn't with his wife that night, either. As a matter of fact, he introduced who he was with, after all, we were all in this church thing together, under the same 'covering'…a whore covering.

The pastor and his wife were aware of this long term relationship this brother was having with another married member. Now, ain't that some covering up of laying on hands?

LoveLife's final blow was the dinner the First Lady (pastor's wife) invited her to. She wanted to clear the air, and see where LoveLife's head was at, she knew so much was going on in LoveLife's life but it didn't matter to her. She had a role to play, a title to live up to. She was the "first" lady….but she wasn't Bishop PleaseHer only lady. She knew it, she didn't care, she wanted LoveLife's husband.

LoveLife: I can't do this any longer, I'm filing for a divorce and moving on, you have no idea what I'm dealing with. My mind is being attacked, he's constantly doing things to hurt me, mentally. I don't think he'll try putting his hands on me again after I whipped dat ass.

The pastor's wife: Well, what are you doing that's causing him to be the way he is? LoveLife wanted to jump across that table and beat her ass, and ask her, "Bitch, you fucking him or something?"

LoveLife's friend is next to her and she grabs LoveLife's hand under the table and squeezes for dear life to keep her calm.

LoveLife: I allowed myself to travel down this road, I'm good.

I'm not even asking God to deliver me out of this, I'm just asking him to keep me in my right mind because I'm dealing with something vomited up from hell and its mission is to destroy me, I've recognized exactly what I'm dealing with. So to answer your question, I'm doing absolutely nothing outside of what a wife is "supposed" to do. And dwelling with him ain't pleasing.

The pastor's wife: Well, at least discuss this with the Bishop before you make a decision.

Little did the pastor's wife know that the decision was made but LoveLife agreed to consult with Bishop PleaseHer.

His advice after she shared her concerns and fears was, "Can you just sleep in separate rooms and try to work this out?"

LoveLife would do just that, she had been doing that all along.

LoveLife held her peace because she knew this was beyond her marriage to The Mate and this Ministry, and these people were crazy as hell, and had hell all up in 'em.

Her soul screams: LORD, GIVE ME STRENGTH TO REMOVE MYSELF FROM ALL OF THIS FOOLISHNESS I ALLOWED, I WON'T ASK YOU TO REMOVE ME OR HELP ME, BECAUSE I DID THIS! I ALLOWED THIS! JUST GIVE ME STRENGTH TO DO WHAT I NEED TO DO TO DELIVER MYSELF FROM THE SITUATIONS I'VE ALLOWED. THIS HELL I WALKED INTO. I WENT INTO ALL OF THIS AND STAYED WITH MY EYES WIDE OPEN. Lord, I heard you when you said, "Daughter, you don't have to do this, don't marry him, don't walk out there, just send the guest home, he'll get over the embarrassment. Walk away now."

That's why I can only cry for strength because I ignored your warning. Lord, I repent. Forgive me for ignoring your directions.

LoveLife went on with her decision to separate herself from her mentally abusive mate and removed herself from the congregation of crazy after several emotional and very traumatic alterations.

LoveLife would lose a lot during her divorce but she gained herself back, her dignity, her peace, her life, gained it all back.

She'd remain "Ministry Friends" with that church and Bishop PleaseHer and his wife. It wasn't real though, it was just what humans do. LoveLife would hear the stories of all of the covers being pulled off of a lot of the things going on there, but she was pleased not to be apart while sad to know that things were so dysfunctional. And for whatever reason, Bishop PleaseHer had to try a few years later to see if he could get LoveLife to bite his sexual invite....

After ignoring his invitation to, "How many licks is that?" he'd stop by her workplace while she was outside on a break. He saw her and wanted her to see him in his very luxury ride...LoveLife wasn't not moved. She lived in a material world but wasn't a material girl. She could smell the lust in the air, and saw the lust in his eyes. She said to him: Oh, pastors riding like that now?

He replied, " a little something…" She made it known that she had millionaire and billionaire friends that also drove that type of "lil something" he pulled up in.

"Need any help, looks like you're moving boxes?" he would ask.

LoveLife declined his offer to help.

And she walked off, leaving him in his thirst.

There was something about a thirsty man wanting what he wanted simply because he couldn't have it. Maybe it was the lies told by her then husband, had Bishop PleaseHer thinking LoveLife was a freak.

I've experienced and heard so many stories from so many individuals trusting folks that "come in the name of the Lord." The bible says to let God be true and every person a lie, to search the scriptures for yourself to rightly divide the word of truth.

I've experienced so much destruction in ministries and cults and groups and churches and families and companies and commitments because of a lack of knowledge or because they're afraid to follow the leading and direction of their soul, their intuition. We attend and join these organized organizations and lose self, we lose soul, we lose our voice. We lose our I am. The God in us.

We'll allow them to imprison us with scriptures like, "What profiteth a man to gain the whole world and lose his soul?."

While we watch them gain all of our "tithes and offerings.." Gaining houses, land, stocks, bonds, boats, cars, and more cars. Watching single women being taken advantage of thinking she the anointed one, the called one, the Teddy PendeLAYherASS down one. "Come on and go with me, come on over to my place."

We allow these uncalled "called by God " lost souls into our lives by way of their sermons, their bible studies....their seminars, counseling their beliefs on us and not seeking God's direction, we allow them in and lose our families, our way, our selves....our celibacy, and our "till death do us part."When the uncalled sees you've committed all of your trust and money to them, and the most valuable commodity of all, time, they get comfortable with you and seek more because they feel your weakness for their manmade righteousness is their open door to see if you're willing to partake in their secret life, their lust for sex life, regardless your gender. Some of them have a required taste, an Oscar Myers taste. They know you're not trusting or seeking direction from your soul's point of view any longer, all of the meetings and counseling sessions you make appointments for are a dead giveaway, it's obvious to them you seek to please them. You've muted your soul's scream and they recognize that you've given up your soul right, and that right is to know everyone by their spirit.

Question everyone and everything.

Believe nothing you hear with your human ears, hear it and evaluate it with your spiritual ear.

Stop silencing your intuition. That's your soul protecting you.

Don't allow what you see with your human vision to deceive what you see with your soul vision.

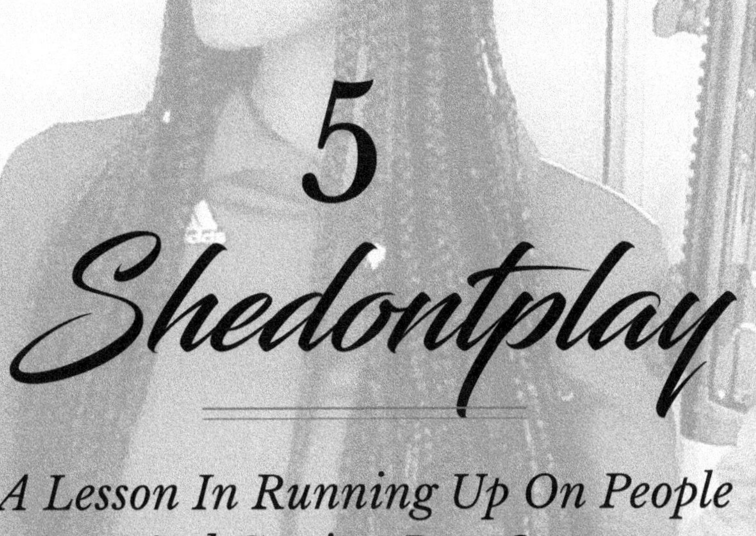

5
Shedontplay
A Lesson In Running Up On People
And Getting Ran Over

"You're gonna be with me, watch! I like what I see and you'll be with me."

McCleanny stepped to Shedontplay that cold day in December as she was leaving the hospital, and went to visit her peeps that were healing from some hard knocks. She was exiting the hospital to catch up with her DJ to pay him for the New Years Event she was planning. Out of nowhere, walking out the hospital doors, McCleanny runs up to her like he knows her. She was thrown and nervous but she stopped in her tracks.

"Hi beautiful, I'm McCleanny and I'm your next relationship, your last relationship, and your soon to be husband."

Shedontplay stood there and just laughed but she listened while he went on. She thinks, does this dude know me, how does he know I'm single?

Then she interrupts him and says,

"I tell you what, Mccleanny, give me your number and I'll send you the information for the party next week." They exchange numbers.

As promised, she contacted him with the party details, and he showed up with the same energy he exchanged with her at the hospital and they had a great time. He asked if he could see Shedontplay again, take her out…she was down with a date, since she was single and happy about it.

For the next few months, they dated and chilled, everything was good. Everything! Shedontplay was learning to be sexually free.

McCleanny's romance was so good that she decided to have a house party at her place and introduce him. He was excited about meeting some of her crew, after all she met his daughter and a couple of cousin's so why not, they were spending a lot of time together, and things were good. Sex was good good. Shedontplay wasn't looking for anything serious but McCleanny was and he made it known in his actions.

The party day comes, the guest arrives but McCleanny never makes the party and he never calls, he's not answering the phone. Shedontplay ain't sweatin it but she's hoping he's ok.

He calls the next day explaining his situation, "Hey babe, I was locked up and with it being on a Saturday, I had to wait till Monday to bail out.". McCleanny is from a small town so Shedontplay didn't question it but she became suspicious because she'd been through the shit talk before and shit didn't sound right.

She decided to take a ride to his place, after all, he gave her keys and she was always there. Shedontplay pulled up and his truck was out front. Hmm, she thought.

She took her keys out and opened the door…

He was there and she was there. Who in da hell was this? Shedontplay thought to herself.

He was drunk and passed out on the sofa…

The woman was sitting there, looking shocked to see

someone opening the door, and it's obvious that she's upset because he's out and she's up, looking at the TV and holding onto her overnight bag.

Shedontplay: Who are you?

The Woman: I'm…

Shedontplay: What's going on here?

The Woman: McCleanny picked me up to spend the weekend with him…

Shedontplay: Is that so….

Shedontplay makes her way over to the sofa to wake the sleeping whore, McCleanny.

Shedontplay: Wake the fuck up!

McCleanny: What…that's my cousin, she needed a place to stay…Shedontplay looks at Young and Dumb and gives her the 'sistercode' look. Shedontplay knows better.

Her soul screams: STAY CALM AND BREATHE. COUNT….ANYTHING TO KEEP US OUT OF JAIL TONIGHT. LEAVE! Shedontplay, WE GOT THIS QUEEN, HE AIN'T WORTH IT, BREATH QUEEN, BREATHE. DON'T GIVE HIM YOUR ENERGY. WE CAN SAGE HIS ASS RIGHT OUT OF OUR LIFE…JUST WALK AWAY.

Shedontplay ignored her soul's cry…….

She goes in and it is ugly! McCleanny calls the cops, Shedontplay waits for the cops and she is still going in on McCleanny, the woman is still sitting on the sofa, shocked and stiff like a mannequin.

The cops arrive.

Immediately, McCleanny plays the victim, and it's obvious he was the "victim" because Shedontplay pounced on him like he was a wide receiver getting tackled.

He asked the cops to please remove her from his home. She was shocked, she was in a daze, lost and confused.

"Is this really happening, McCleanny? For real? The police? You ain't man enough to finish what you started, too weak to clean up yo mess? You good with let'n the police finish ya lil dirty work?"

Shedontplay screams at McCleanny while being removed from his house by the police.

The cops asked Shedontplay to please leave, and McCleanny yelled, "Wait!" Shedontplay kept walking, "Ask her for the key before she leaves please, I want my key," Oh punk ass Mccleany cries to the police. "She may come back and I don't want any problems." He knew she was coming back, she had asked him for her art back.

She gives him a key, not his key though.

For whatever reason, McCleanny knew the key was the wrong one but Shedontplay had made her escape. McCleanny must have known that Shedontplay, don't play.

McCleanny had to be to work early in the morning, like four a.m.

Shedontplay had called up her troops, she'd been plotting, thinking up a master plan, she needed some movers, she was about to shake his world…

Her troop answered the call, they took a truck and her sister's car as she couldn't take hers because she didn't want to be recognized by the neighbors, and the police.

While Mccleanny was on his way to work, Shedontplay was on her way to his house, to clean out the house.

Baby, listen… Shedontplay had her troops go in and clean out his apartment. They took everything not locked down, she took the food out of the freezer, the toilet tissue off the holder… everything. She had no intention of cleaning out his home. Her intent was to take what she'd just shared with him a few days prior to all of the deception, her art.

She'd just purchased him two beautiful works of art, so she really went back to take what was hers, her expression of love. Shedontplay was an art collector, that was her thing. Gifting you with art was her way of showing you that you'd gifted her with something special and it didn't have to be materialistic. Gifting you with art was her way of expressing her love for you, her care. It expressed that you had touched her heart, her soul in some special way.

When he realized she'd given him the wrong key, he put the art she wanted back in his truck and took them to work with him. He had no idea the brilliance of this woman he jumped in front of all those few months ago, had he known, he would've respected the game and not allowed himself to be played.

One of her troopers asked, "Cuz, whose apartment is this?"

Shedontplay replied, "Some stupid ass who tried me, nigga."

The trooper said, "Oh" and kept loading the truck.

The other trooper was like, "Man, to be a fly on this wall when dis nigga gets home."

"Take those speakers, the tv, his lil DVD player and DVD's, take it all," Shedontplay said with pride.

They cleaned the house. The only thing she left was a naked bed for him to sleep on and his precious achievements. They drove back to town and loaded up a single mom's home that Shedontplay knew. She told the mom that night, "Bring me your keys, you'll have some gifts waiting for you when you get home."

McCleanny never reached out to Shedontplay, she never heard from him….he knew he'd F'd up.

Shedontplay wasn't done, so she woke up early the next day and took one last personal trip to McCleanny's place. She used her key one final time, she entered, it was thick in the air that he knew he'd tried the wrong one…that huge cheap jug of wine sitting on the toilet tank was a solid indication he'd had been home and was in pain. She could clearly see the image in her head, and she laughed.

Shedontplay left him one last solid reminder of who she was, she took a knife and shredded his mattress into confetti.

"Now it is finished," Shedontplay said and walked out, leaving the door wide open.

It would be years later before Shedontplay would hear from Mccleanny again….

Phone rings:

Shedontplay: Hello.

Mccleanny: Hey…

Shedontplay: Who is this?

Mccleanny: It's me, Mccleanny.

Shedontplay: Get off my damn phone, oh hoe asss, punk ass, sorry ass. He yelled, "Why I gotta be all that?."

Shedontplay hung up in disbelief but laughed to herself and heard a gentle whisper from her soul, "When it's good, it just is…"

The way Shedontplay drugged him, Mccleany should have lost all of her information when he came home to an empty house all those years ago.

Her soul would scream with laughter thinking about the vengeance, how good it actually felt to play a role in Mccleany's karma.

Soul Lesson:

It's so freaking easy to be true, fair and honest in these relationships. If it's a sexual attraction with no plans for anything further, come out the gate with that. You never know, she just may wanna get her freak on as well. What's not fair is your lie that sets her up to lie to herself. She starts lying to herself because of what you fed her. Your, "I gotta have her sexually," lie. The seemingly convincing lies that bring her to trust what you're offering. She'll see your lies coming a mile away but will believe what you spit. Just keep the playing field one hundred. Two actually can play that game. Honesty is a great relationship policy. If it was just for play, just say that. There's nothing wrong with grown folks playing in each other's sandboxes. Toys can be shared then you can take yo ass home....take your toys, though, don't leave nothing in her sandbox, get yo shit out his sandbox and go home....don't play ya self. Run up on the right playa and get knocked da fudge out....
Just remember, swings just ain't a playground term anymore. Make sure you're bout that life....though. Don't get beat at your own game. Lay all the terms on the table.
Have your soul saying "Oh, heart, stop making a fool out of us."

6

Churchy

A Lesson In Searching The Scriptures For Your Damn Self

"I know you'll do extremely well wherever you go, I understand it's time for you to move on from this ministry if you believe the Lord is telling you to move, we will miss you but you must do what the Lord is telling you to do."

That was the farewell Churchy received when she had a meeting with the Pastor of the church she'd been a member of for over thirteen years.

Churchy left in peace, or so she'd thought. She had been trying to get out of that cult for a couple of years, especially after that she'd come under their radar because she decided to divorce her husband. She was advised to stay in the marriage and try to work it out, even when she shared that her then husband wanted to get rid of her, and she knew well that domestic abuse and violence wasn't always body bruises being visible.

"I don't think he meant he wanted to kill you, give him a chance, he's a great guy." That was the advice given, and so Churchy knew it was time to go. Even she knew the warning always came before the destruction. Yes, her then husband wanted to blow her brains out because she no longer wanted to be in a marriage where she was the only one married. Her husband's definition of marriage was providing a roof, lights, food, bills to be paid and a car to drive, as long as he could still give his penis to these hoes in the streets.

Churchy was tired of competing with street Coochie, and knew it was time to file for a divorce, so she started doing the most to feel loved, outside of her marriage. She'd find herself entertaining the lust demon her husband introduced to their holy union.

When the elders, especially the men, of her church home became aware of Churchy's decision to divorce her husband, they began to attack her, she'd be approached from here and there. "Your outfit is beautiful but that skirt is a little too high to be sitting on the front row, maybe you should move back a few rows…"

That was written on a note passed to her by one of the ushers from the pulpit. She took the note and moved right out the door, heading home. She was done, but was stopped and asked to stay. "Don't let them make you run away," she would be told. She stayed for the remainder of the service because she knew she had zero points to prove. She knew it was time to go when she scanned the front row of knees and thighs and short dresses on display. She was a tiny something, not desiring any of the men up in that place and they were worried about her lil knees and legs popping. It was time for her to make her exit. She knew she was being spiritually attacked. God the Father, Son nor The Holy Spirit was involved in this mission to break Churchy's big, bold and confident spirit.

She realized she was being targeted.

One Sunday she sat in the back and watched the pastor come out, the choir and congregation stood and begin to sing. Churchy used to participate in this scene because it seemed so very innocent, but this Sunday would be different. She stood but she felt convicted because she realized they were worshipping this pastor.

Maybe that's why they started paying attention to her because shortly after that, she would stand no more. She would try her best to be a part of the ministry, just attend and go home, no more activities, no more anything. This ministry was all she knew since salvation so she felt that surely God made no mistakes and it was 'the devil' telling her to leave. The voice was clear and comforting but when you don't study and learn for yourself how to rightly divide the truth, or when you're spoiled from being spoon fed, you'll question the god in you because you're told he will not speak to you without speaking to your 'anointed pastor' first.

So, you sit in spiritual fear because you haven't been taught to learn to hear the spirit for yourself. But God!

How great thou art…

How great thou art…

God began to thorn the nest, and Churchy was being prepared to fly, and with every service she had become more uncomfortable. She'd watch beautiful spirits being destroyed "in the name of the anointing" because of human experiences as their bodies would show the evidence of their "backsliding" moments. Churchy was different because she knew the backstory of so many of those now pointing their salvation fingers at the "fallen."

She was exhausted from sitting in the midst of the over critical congregation. Churchy would receive her spiritual strength and have that exit conversation with the pastor and leave.

That Monday, the news had traveled fast that Churchy had left the Lord. Not the Church she had fellowship and tithed into for thirteen years, it was said she'd left Salvation. She had backslid. Her hands were wicked, she wasn't to be trusted, she hated the pastor, and Churchy was made out to be a demon like none other. She would get her first taste of this deception as she listened to the lies told about her that same day.

Dropping her baby off to the daycare, Churchy would hear, "Oh, the daycare is good enough for her child but the church ain't good for her."

That would be the last time she'd drop her baby off.

Churchy was a business woman, and most of her business was from this church. Business was good and blessed. The week went by and Churchy was clueless that an entire meeting had taken place concerning her leaving the church.

The leaders were told to pull aside all of the individuals they knew were customers of Churchy and have them make a conscious decision 'on their own' to stop patronizing Churchy's establishment. It worked, and Saturday would come and her regulars would come through but her church crowd was missing.

She didn't think anything of it because she was busy. Something hit her though, that her assistant wasn't there, so she rang them.

THE CONVERSATION:

(Phone rings and is answered.)

The assistant: Hello.

Churchy: Hey, are you coming in today? It's getting busy, and I'm getting backed up.

The Assistant: no ma'am, I can't assist you anymore, I'm not allowed to come back up there.

Churchy: Why? What's up? Did I do something wrong? Churchy was hurt behind this because this kid was her heart, she adored this kid.

The Assistant: No ma'am, I was told you are a bad influence for me to be around, I can't be around you anymore. You could hear the hurt in the assistant's voice, as they knew better but were under aged and under the influence of the adults caring for them.

Churchy: Is this because I left the church? Whoever told you this is a liar, I spoke with the pastor and it is well. Who told you this?

The Assistant: The pastor did.

Her soul screams: OH MY GOD! WHAT IS GOING ON! DID I REALLY HEAR WHAT I JUST HEARD? THIS PASTOR IS LYING ON ME. THIS CAN'T BE TRUE. LORD AVENGE ME OF ALL OF MY ENEMIES, I CRIED OUT. HOW DO I DEAL WITH THIS, THIS IS SPIRITUAL, THIS

IS NEW TO ME. TO BE DECEIVED AND ATTACKED BY THOSE I WOULD NEVER THINK COULD DO SUCH A THING. WHAT KIND OF NEW HELL IS THIS?

Churchy: Well, I'll miss you and I understand, you're a young adult and you must do what you're told because you're still living at home but know this, you were told a lie.

The following Saturday came around, and it'd been a rough week for Churchy because she didn't know what to make of all of this. After all, she was set for years and would see the individual leave and they'd be "preached" on from that pit. She never shunned anyone because if she wasn't aware of anything else, she was sure of this very thing, that it wasn't "Godly" to shun, ignore, avoid and judge individuals because they'd made a godly decision to leave a church, particularly this church. Churchy never got down with that cultish belief so when it was her turn, she was disturbed by it because she knew she'd done it the 'correct' way. She knew she'd continued to sow seeds of love, regardless of the hate that would be ministered from that pulpit sometimes. It was disturbing but Churchy knew humans were doing Godly deeds to the best of their ability based on what they believed.

Knowing all of this history, Churchy still made the decision to leave in peace, don't just leave. Not that it mattered. At least they were not a respect of persons. They preached on her and ignored her in public places just like they'd done to so many before her.

The committed church members started missing appointments with Churchy. It was very clear to Churchy that the imps had reached all of her customers and filled them with an 'ungodly fear…' a very ugly untruth.

"How are you going to continue to support a business that hates your pastor?" They'd try to poison the minds of the ones that made their personal "free indeed" decision to remain customers with Churchy.

Churchy would be preached on for a long time. Beautiful relationships would be disrupted (the real ones eventually came around) and people were literally afraid of Churchy because of what was being said about her from the pit.

She recalls a few soldiers though, they stood their ground and continued to remain friends with Churchy and would support her business. One was so supportive that she was clueless that the pastor was the one throwing rocks and hiding hands. "I'm going to talk with the pastor because those leaders around here telling us not to support your business, talking 'bout your hands are wicked." Churchy didn't want to disappoint her so she didn't share what she knew for sure.

Eventually, Churchy would move on from the hurt and the pain of that backstabbing. She was introduced to church hurt for the first time in her life. She realized it was a different kind of hurt. She didn't feel this pain with a cheating mate so she was aware that things done to you spiritually was a type of witchcraft. It pains you differently. Even with marriage being a "holy matrimony," because it's obvious that God ain't joining a lot of these marriages together, she didn't feel this kind of anger. She thought of so many ways to retaliate, to clear her name with this small group of followers, but she knew it wasn't for her to handle. Her soul would scream out to her, "ALLOW GOD TO AVENGE YOU, THIS IS TOO BIG FOR YOU."

She'd listen to the leading of her soul.

She'd had an encounter with one of the former leaders from that place, where the leader apologized to Churchy. Actually, this took place a few times. It was a cycle of former leaders and members apologizing This particular ex-leader wanted Churchy to sue the pastor for defamation of character, the ex-leaders were willing to write a letter proving defamation of character and were willing to testify because they were ear and eyewitnesses to the verbal destruction and lies that flowed from this pastor's mouth. They witnessed the harm it caused Churchy's business as well as the number of customers she lost because the church members were "encouraged" to no longer patronize Churchy.

Churchy declined the offer, she saw what God was doing. She knew those individuals making the decision to leave this cult was God's way of saying what needed to be said without Churchy saying a word to clear the lies that'd been preached about her.

What a mighty God we serve!

Churchy's business would remain steady and her money grew more, regardless of the customer cut.

With an entire 'church' against her, God had her.

Even with Churchy no longer in attendance, the pastor continued her lies. She called Churchy's new pastor. "I see you got that whore over there with you, watch your men and especially your married men, she'll go through them."

She had the new pastor so nervous that they asked God, "Why did you send that hoe over here?"

The pastor would watch and wait on the 'Jezebel' spirit to take over. Waiting on Churchy to have an exorcism moment.

All he could see was the god in her.

Eventually, Churchy would move on from there as well.

Whatever happened to Churchy? She's doing just fine and God is pleased with her.

She'd often joke with her friends that she was going to scream from a bull horn on the back of a truck on a Sunday morning in that church's parking lot, "Let those people go!" She never did. Like the title of the song says and the lyrics sing why "Ghetto kids don't believe in God" by Freddie Bricks.

Soul Lesson

We're always being taught and ministered to about soul ties. We never consider these ties being possible with bishops, pastors, ministers, church leaders,etc. We give these average humans too much credit. Those of us going to confession asking a man to forgive us because we've sinned. The counseling we seek from these average humans, asking them advice about our personal lives, our marriages, and our children. We're creating soul ties. God said to acknowledge Him in all our ways, he'll direct our path. Instead, we seek direction from these average humans, creating little gods in our spiritual lives. We seek the god in them before we trust the God in us, our trusted intuition.

I remember one church goer suggesting that I don't allow my children to "visit" their dad on his scheduled weekends. "Is he saved?" she asked me . I just stared at her. Different church, different pitcher of kool aid. We may not admit it but we know we've messed up our children with the unprofessional advice we've applied to their upbringing from these pulpit bullies who destroy their self esteem and their direction. We are good at repeating "what passda said" and not what God is saying or has said.

We have to stop pushing this drug called religion. Salvation is freedom, hell, it's free. We've poured so much into these organized weapons of spiritual destruction until we've become numb to the common sense of who God really is. He is love. Without love we have nothing. We shouldn't be following anything that's teaching us it's greater than the God in US. It's an unhealthy doctrine that they want us to think is normal. What church are you a member of?" Member? Is God about members now or is he about the people? It's no longer about the people, it's about the one that told you God called them. We should never be good with being comfortable with being spiritually soul tied to anything or anyone that's comfortable with manipulating the people of God or destroying people and relationships from the pulpits.

7

Essence

When They Do Not Travel Well With Themselves, They Won't Travel Well With You

"You've never been to the Essence festival? Every black person should attend it at least once!"

The Essence festival is Ebonee's thing. She plans her trip every year, she hasn't been home for a fourth of July in years. The festival always takes place around the fourth. Every year, she invites a crew to travel with her, but it doesn't matter if they go or not because she knows how to party. If anyone shows themselves as party poopers, she will remain unphased.

Like that one time she partied with her girlfriend and she met the fireman. They hung out and enjoyed the activities until his side piece danced up on them at the club and showed out. The side piece had uninvitedly followed him to New Orleans. He hung out with his boys while his wife was at home. The fireman told her the woman was just a side chick, basically a stalker because she'd traveled all the way to New Orleans assuming her fireman would house her in his hotel room since the hotels were booked all the way over to Mississippi. He left her in the lobby with nowhere to lay her head. Chance would set it up for Ebonee to be the fireman's hotel room neighbor. He was cute and Ebonee was single. Clueless about the stalker, Ebonee noticed the fireman on his balcony they shared.

They spark up a conversation and Ebonee informs the fireman that this is her tenth festival. It is his first so he's looking forward to her helping him maneuver around the city as he is excited to participate in all of the festivities New Orleans has to offer. They met up at one of the clubs later that evening, each of them accompanied by their roommate. He asked Ebonee to dance.

Someone danced up on them and pushed Ebonee.

It's the stalker.

The fireman told the stalker to go, "Move wit yo crazy ass, don't bring that shit all the way to New Orleans, I told you I don't fuck wit yo ass no mo. "

Ebonee just stepped back, assuming the stalker was his wife because she came up on them like she was wearing his last name.

"She ain't my wife, she's this chick I used to mess with back home, she followed me here," the fireman shares with Ebonee.

"Oh, so she's a chick on the side?" Ebonee said.

"Well, is there a wife?" Ebonee went on to ask. "I'll respect the wife but I ain't respecting no side piece."

The fireman was honest, "Yes, but we're not together. It's simple, she caught me fudging around with her, the stalker, and she left me."

"Oh, ok," Ebonee said.

Ebonee continued to dance until she danced ole girl out the way. She was determined to enjoy her evening.

Ebonee thinks to herself as she's dancing and being eyeballed by her stalker:*Girl, get a grip. You followed this borrowed penis all the way out of town with nowhere to lay your head, he won't even give you the time of day. You can't even get a dance, not even a pillow for you to sleep in the hallway and you running up on me like that? Like this yo husband? Girl, you are making all kinds of fools out of yourself.*

The side piece sat in the corner hopelessly staring at us dancing the night away. Ebonee made sure to work the fireman over. She worked him out on that dance floor. She wanted to send the side piece a message. With her dance moves, Ebonee taught the side piece a very valuable lesson. A married man will lay and play. He may love his wife but if he's a whore in these streets and you're the reason his wife leaves him, he will be done playing with you once the fun fades. The only power your coochie got is side piece power. It's not strong enough to make a man stay. He'd rather take a chance and get another. He would try his chances with Ebonee, thinking his honesty was key, it was. It gave Ebonee power. She enjoyed Mr. Fireman but she respected the wife, even though she dumped his ass, she wasn't going to divorce him. She did however, give him some time in the streets while she entertained someone else blowing out her fire.

Another trip Ebonee remembered was when she accompanied Mr. Insecure to a Kem concert. Ebonee was in a zone. Infatuated by this handsome, black artist, Ebonee found herself in a daze as she was singing and gazing into the eyes of her favorite artist. Last year, she was introduced to Kem by Mr. Insecure at one of the Super Lounge's. She fell in love with the beautiful black man and his music. That first year, Mr Insecure enjoyed watching Ebonee enjoy Kem. He was happy that she finally agreed with him on something. Ebonee was simple but by the way she carried herself, men would think differently, like she was immortal; a goddess. It was considered a compliment to them when Ebonee would show them special attention. Mr Insecure finally received his compliment, his stamp of approval.

What a difference a year will make. You can pretend but it will soon end. Your nature will get tired of being your well kept secret.

The following year, the couple would attend with several other couples. Mr. Insecure was already on the out's with Ebonee, it'd been a year from hell. She was trying so hard to make it work. She ignored all of the "do not enter this disaster zone" warning lights.

Mr. Insecure was a work of dysfunction, Ebonee had never experienced that type of deceitful wickedness in all her days. This dude was recording her phone calls, hiding her poetry books and trying his best to destroy her relationship with her children. Mr. Insecure was jealous of everything that was a part of Ebonee. If she loved it, he was questioning it. He'd even convinced himself she was having an affair with the guy down the sidewalk from her business because every time she'd look out the door, she was looking for her "lover" He was so convinced of this that he even shared this lie with some of her customers.

"See, look, she always going to the door looking down there

at her nigga, she ain't fooling me," he'd try to convince her customers.

Her customers cared not to share this with Ebonee because her customers knew better so they knew how Ebonee would respond. They waited until the divorce was over and verbally drug his ass through the ground. They told her everything. She was so embarrassed.

Back to the concert. This year Kem was on the mainstage because he'd killed the super lounge last year with his performance. They were in there like sardines and pork-n-beans, both shows, so they featured him on the mainstage to accommodate the fans. It was nice but Ebonee preferred seeing Kem up close and personal. He's that kind of performer, according to her.

Sitting there and enjoying Kem, Mr. Insecure whispered in Ebonee's ear, "I wish you could feel for me the same way you do about Kem."

One of the couples was in hearing range and leaned over and asked, "Is he serious? Did I just hear him say that?"

Embarrassed, Ebonee replied, "Yes, he's really being himself on this trip and this will be his last festival with me. This is only a small scale of what I go through."

Her girlfriend was so upset and hurt for Ebonee because she peeped a few things but she thought she was imagining Ebonee's mate having a weird vibe. Nope. Unfortunately, she was seeing what Ebonee could no longer hide, her sad and pitiful self pretending to be in a loving marriage.

Ebonee would fake it through the remainder of this trip because other couples were accompanying them. That would be the last time Ebonee would see Kem and Mr. Insecure at the Essence festival.

Her soul screams: LOVE YOURSELF SO FIERCELY AND SO UNAPOLOGETICALLY THAT YOU HAVE NO ROOM FOR INSECURE INDIVIDUALS TO FILL IN ANY CRACKS THEY MAY FIND IN YOUR FOUNDATION. I'M SETTLED AND THOSE CRACKS ARE THERE BECAUSE OF IT.

Let's share another Essence adventure:

A few years later, Ebonee was dating again and she took her new boo on her annual Essence Trip. His excitement made her even more excited about the festival. This was his first experience there, so she popped his essence cherry. He was a kid in a candy shop. Ebonee couldn't believe he'd never been to this festival. He'd shared how his ex wife and his buddies would attend every year, so he knew about Essence but was never invited. Man, his soul should've been speaking to him in Ebonics, he should've been questioning why he was never extended an invite to travel to this Essence from the individuals who were such a huge part of his life. I'm sure his soul was screaming foul.

Ebonee knew the rules, she knew that what went on at

Essence, stayed at Essence. It was like Las Vegas taking over New Orleans but you had to have your black card.

Eventually, the two would attend the festival as a couple. One special year would end up being their Honeymoon Essence.

Her once a year get away became their annual get away.

Essence isn't a secret to keep, Ebonee felt every black person should experience it at least once in their life., She felt so strongly about it that she even took her children to experience it. She never did that again. She realized this was her baby, her me time not to be shared with kids.

When her me time turned into their we time, the couple decided to invite other married couples along. Ebonee loved and appreciated their unions. A few bumps would take place, you never knew what to expect having so many different energies in a closed yet shared space. The kinks would work themselves out though and it ended up being one of the best couple trips Ebonee would experience.

Ebonee would learn a great deal from her many excursions to the Essence Festivals. This environment helped her to appreciate being a black woman. She appreciated seeing all the black love in one city. She had the best travel agent so she never worried about transportation and rooms. These trips were soul moments for Ebonee. She learned who she really was, her personal triggers and her strengths. Every year would bring on a new lesson.

Traveling is definitely good for the soul.

Traveling allowed Ebonee to hear her soul screams in a different tone, the screams would be calmer and clearer. She craved Essence every year, she craved the moments she could be in the presence of so many melanin shades of people and experience black culture from the moment she'd walk on the bus and take her seat. Essence was her Africa. She loved all things Black Culture.

Ebonee still travels to her favorite festival, and it never gets old to her because it feeds and rejuvenates her soul. She eventually came to the realization that Essence was a vibe, a black experience that couldn't be shared or appreciated by all simply because you are black. She overstood that even though Essence is a black thing, all black skin didn't overstand. They could only understand from their childlike perspective.

Never change your standards to accommodate what makes you uncomfortable. Respect isn't necessarily given when it's not demanded. Hell, even when it's demanded, it may be challenged. So learn to respect the time you've set aside to relax your mind. Relate to yourself and release the troubles or worries you can't physically do anything about. You can't do anything about it anyway. Grant yourself permission to travel away from those moments, those people and those burdens. Learn that spiritual travel is just as important as physical travel. Learn to understand yourself spiritually, when you travel. Learn to get away, to lay it aside. Learn what your essence is. Allow yourself to travel to where your intuition is leading you. Learn to travel soul light and enjoy those moments. Reconnect with your voice, your soul and ignite your vibe. Can't physically get away? No problem, that's what meditation is for, some call it daydreaming. I think our soul is recalling beautiful moments it wants to revisit or is longing for. So seek a quiet place to meditate and vision yourself in your favorite soul place. Vacation there as long as necessary. The only thing this type of vacation will cost is your time. It'll be the best time commodity you've ever spent.

8

Sugaraya

A Lesson In Don't Start None Won't Be None

"Can I dance with your husband?" CoCo would ask SugaRaya as she held SugaRaya's husband's hand and pulled on him to dance to a slow song. This was at the birthday party SugaRaya was throwing for her handsome husband, East.

All eyes were on SugaRaya as everyone was awaiting her answer. Still holding East's hand, CoCo assumed it would be fine. East was looking crazy because he was drunk. Not completely drunk, he just knew what was about to unfold. He was sober enough to just stand there while CoCo made a fool of herself. Waiting on a yes SugaRaya thought to herself, *'Bitch what!* As she stared at CoCo, CoCo realized she didn't need an interpreter to understand the loud "Hell no," that SugaRaya was saying with her eyes.

Shocked and disturbed, CoCo dropped East's hands. CoCo was one of the girls from the tailgate. East and his boys would get together every home game and throw a big event. This was something he engaged in before he met SugaRaya so she was aware of the Sunday tradition, but what she wasn't aware of was the little pet names the women called themselves there… Names like tailgate wife and tailgate girlfriend. These women would cater to these men, fix plates and drinks and things like that. CoCo was so comfortable with her position as one of these tailgate wives/girlfriends that she forgot she was in the presence of East's actual wife. Well, she didn't forget, she had enough sense to try to attempted to be polite by asking if she could dance with her husband, not realizing she was still overstepping her boundaries. I guess she was so used to dancing with East as his tailgate wife that she became jealous of the attention he was giving his wife at his birthday party. SugaRaya knew to begin to pay attention to this CoCo and she began to question what was really going on at these tailgates. Why was this woman so comfortable asking her to slow dance with her husband?

Before SugaRaya married East, she attended a couple of the tailgates with him, she sat and observed. She would soon discover that the tailgate life wasn't for her but East was committed to them. It was apparent that most of the women were single and most of the men were married or dating. At the time she didn't question it because she and East were only dating. The football season was coming to its end and East was planning his big super bowl event, the tailgate finale. Normally, the tailgate crew would get together and chip in and fund the final event. That year, the guys decided to go all out and not include the tailgate "wives and girlfriends". East agreed and shared this information with SugaRaya. She was cool with it, she helped East prepare for his big event and she left.

While she was leaving, the tailgate wives and girlfriends started showing up, and SugaRaya looked at East as she headed out and just shook her head, but she gave East the look that spoke volumes.

East begged her to stay because he already knew the evening

was done, and how would he explain this to SugaRaya? The guys had set him up and it wasn't a good look, especially with him wanting to move his relationship with SugaRaya to a more serious level. Not "the next level" but just a more serious level. She'd be committed to him completely and he'd be committed to her when it was convenient.

East caught SugaRaya at the door to try to stop her from leaving as his wide eyes grazed hers, he said, "Suga, I had no idea those women were coming. That was not the agreement discussed at the meeting," he said.

Suga just looked at him and said nothing. East asked her to stay, but she was adamant about leaving. "Apparently your crew planned this so I'll respect that. Besides, I've already made plans," she said as she walked off.

Well, in the third quarter, SugaRaya decided to swing by the "all boys" event. Needless to say, women were wall to wall. East was tending to the bar. Suga walked over and greeted him, and he seemed relieved. He smiled because he knew what type of woman he was dating, a beast of a woman. James Brown said, !*Poppa don't take no mess.*"Well, Suga didn't either. As long as they didn't start with her, there wouldn't be any reason for her to act like a beast.

It would end up being another successful superbowl event but there was one issue still sitting and waiting on East's attention, a tailgate/superbowl honey was dragging her heels, taking her sweet time to leave. She wanted to be East's touchdown for the night, and she wanted to reward East with a superbowl ring.

Suga was waiting for her to leave and she was doing the same. She was real comfortable and sure of herself. I'm guessing she was in her tailgate wife zone because the new girlfriend wasn't around. Call it a woman's intuition.

Suga took East outside and let him have it! She went on about how his homie's disrespected their relationship by bringing other females around in their "all boys" tailgate. She assured him that they wouldn't have allowed that at their homes nor around their committed relationships. Suga demanded to know where she stood in his life and why that foot dragger was still hanging around. Afterall, all of the other women had gone for the night. East did his best to explain his position. So much so that one of his boys was trying his best to help him explain. "SugaRaya, lil honey here with me, that's my girl," his friend said.

That made her even more enraged because this tailgate gathering was now spinning back, full circle onto SugaRaya.

She went back into the house because she was demanding answers. The boys were sitting and looking reckless because they all had a front seat to the movie premier of 'SugaRaya Don't Play That."

She was boiling hot and it was obvious. East couldn't take the embarrassment of it all so he left. Suga wasn't done because tailgate honey was still lingering waiting on East to dismiss

SugaRaya. Miss TailGate sat there, so sure of her position, afterall, she was the honey he was licking on at the tailgates.

Angry with the TailGate crew, SugaRaya eventually went in on everyone, and spoke her mind to every man in the room, the boys that "had East's back..."

One shouted out:

"Who da fuck you talk'n to?"

"I'm talking to whoever da fuck this applies to!" she angrily responded.

Suga stared at him intensely as she responded. Without another word, East's friend stormed out of the door.

SugaRaya left after the heated exchange, leaving East and his boys in the house with Miss TailGate.

After that lil round in the ring, it was apparent to tailgate honey that she should leave. Suga was sitting in her car, waiting, making sure she saw that lil sports car leave. Suga left shortly after.

SugaRaya was deeply hurt because it became clear to her what kind of bromance she'd be dealing with in this relationship.

On her ride home, her soul was loud, she couldn't silence the scream. She wasn't ready to release the emotion she was truly feeling inside. She tried to hold in her scream but her soul wouldn't allow her to.

Her soul SOUL SCREAMS:

ENOUGH OF THIS CHILDISH SHIT! LET THE

RELATIONSHIP GO. IT'S CLEAR WHERE HE STANDS. THIS ISN'T A MAN OF MORALS AND HE'LL NEVER RESPECT YOU. HE IS A FOLLOWER. FOLLOWING NIGGAS THAT AIN'T TRYING TO HAVE SHIT WHO ALLOWS OTHERS TO JEOPARDIZE HIS SHIT. THEY USE HIS HOME AS THEIR TAILGATE MAN CAVE. YOU EXPERIENCED WHO HE REALLY IS TONIGHT. LET HIM GO! THOSE TAILGATE HONEYS CAN HAVE HIM.

SugaRaya had a lot to sort out. See, this wouldn't be the first encounter with this particular honey. Anytime she was around, she was seeking attention from East. After a while, the situation was hilarious.

SugaRaya recalled one incident where this same chick would be peeping around the cabinets and walls trying to get East's attention. Suga had absolutely no desire to catch this thirsty, disrespectful chick in violation. The powers that be made sure that SugaRaya had a front seat to see this commotion. No matter where East was, whether it was clubs, cookouts, jazz spots or gatherings, she'd attempt to catch his eye. Unfortunately for her, the only eye she'd catch was SugaRaya's death stare. Upon catching it,, tailgate honey would dismiss herself with her head hung low. SugaRaya will never forget the conversation she'd end up having with this particular tailgate honey at East's fortieth birthday bash.

The conversation:

TheTailGateHoney: Suga, may I talk to you for a second?

Suga: Sure…

TheTailGateHoney: I just wanted to thank you for inviting me to the party, I really appreciate it.

(Mind you, Suga didn't invite her. It was assumed she came along with the rest of the tailgate crew or received a special invitation)

Suga: (Looking confused.) No problem. Make sure you eat, there's plenty of food.

TheTailGateHoney: I get it now, I understand. I can see you and East are a couple and I respect that.

Suga figured it was quite twenty/twenty being that East had proposed to SugaRaya and here it was several years later and you're still having to peep through a window when Suga is around because East was good at ignoring her when Suga was present.

Suga didn't give her anything extra. It wasn't even necessary for her to have that "confession talk." . SugaRaya assumed Miss tailgate wanted it to be known that she was the one and this was her way of filing her tailgate divorce from her tailgate husband, East.

SugaRaya just looked at her, feeling absolutely nothing for her, then walked away with a smirk on her face.

SugaRaya's soul would exhale and whisper, "Dis bitch." Two years later and she was still trying to get with East, Suga thought.,

TailGateHoney left shortly after that. Suga figured it was because she couldn't get a rise out of her. What was she expecting SugaRaya to offer her? A "Thank you?"

East is still a lover of all things tailgate, and Suga still 'bitches' about the tailgate events. She sees them as dividers in marriages and relationships. If it's not something that a couple loves to do together, especially the tailgates, East was a part of it. She tried to attend a couple of them but it just wasn't her flavor. She's never been good at faking funks just to fit in .

SugaRaya would always ask East, "What is it about me, why not select to have a relationship with one of the tailgate honeys?"

She knew why, she just wanted him to say it although he never would. Women understand why men don't select a woman to date out of the circle they play in and why they marry outside those circles. SugaRaya understood the unwritten oath.

East would love SugaRaya to the best of his tailgate ability. He knew Suga was good for him but he wasn't ready to sacrifice his commitment to his tailgate family for the good she offered him. East would create the most elaborate lies so he could give that time to them instead.

Suga soon realized she'd wasted enough valuable time ignoring her intuition, and her soul screamed for self-respect. It was time to move on, but East wouldn't agree with breaking up. He'd propose to SugaRaya and all. He fumbled through their relationship, allowed pride and false commitments to superficial things and boys club decrees to sack him. Their relationship went into its final overtime, until eventually, SugaRaya allowed the clock to run out. She'd be done playing herself. She'd be exhausted. She decided it was her turn to call the runs in her life, and she was done with East playing on her field.

My dad will tell you that you have four quarters in life:

First quarter: Birthdate to twenty-five years old.

Second quarter: Twenty-five to fifty years old.

At fifty years old, you've reached your half-time. This is the time for you to regroup and reflect on those things that brought value to your life. This is the time to ask yourself why you fumbled and how you were able to make touchdowns. It's at this time you decide who to keep on your team and who to cut.

Third quarter: Fifty to seventy-five years old. These are your golden years. This is the time when you come off the field and rest. This isn't the time to ride the bench but to provide the practice squad the possibility of remaining on the team and getting called into the game. Give knowledge, wisdom and advice to those willing to listen. to receive your position as the elder, the coach.

If you're blessed to enter your final quarter in life, use this opportunity to play out your entire game of life. Hopefully you can look back and smile because you've made it worth living. No one knows the playbook to their life, we are just given a life. It is imperative that we are taught self-love from the first breath we inhale. We can have nothing if we lack the ability to love.

That's why it's so easy for so many of us to end up being cheated by love, being Miss tailgate, SugaRaya and East. We were taught to play at love, we have to learn to win at love by not playing ourselves because we allow others to play us. Our intuition is there to block all of those plays thrown at us, the ones meant to hinder us when it comes to fake love, convenient love, and we're just afraid to trade those players in thinking no one else will try out for our team. Trust your soul, it already knows what you need and the things you don't. Allow your flesh to ignore those things.

9

Moneybags

A Lesson To Teach Folks To Play With The Lottery Not People, Your Chances Are Better

"Will they be at the cookout? Because I had enough of them last night? I ain't trying to spend my Mother's day looking at that monkey."

This was the question MoneyBags would ask Hotpants when she invited her over for a Mother's Day gathering.

"Will Dr. DegreedNot be at your house for this function?, I'm not entertaining him two nights in a row, I had enough of him last night."

Direct and to the point, the question would be asked. Dr. DegreedNot had a financial debt with MoneyBags, and she wanted her money. She wasn't willing to allow the doctor to sit in her company again and not address the debt he owed her. MoneyBags was willing to respect the doctor's girlfriend and clear the debt but she wasn't willing to make nice with the lying dirt bag that introduced himself as an engineer before he magically became a doctor.

"No, they're not coming," HotPants would lie and say.

"Okay, count me in, I'm on my way," MoneyBags would reply.

It was a beautiful day and MoneyBags was ready to enjoy her Mother's Day. She was the type of mom that didn't celebrate certain calendar days. She understood that most days were created to stimulate the economy, Mother's Day being one of them to her.

Her children were grown and were parent's themselves. She

wasn't the type to pull her elders card and demand her children to shower her with attention, dinner or gifts because the calendar said so. She decided to accept HotPants' invitation for fish and grits.

The night before Mother's Day they were all together at a mutual friend Love Event. Dr. DegreedNot was there with his victim, his girlfriend. MoneyBags was great friends with his girlfriend, at least she thought so. She decided to drop the years-long debt that Dr. DegreedNot owed her. MoneyBags wanted to keep her long-term friendship with the doctor's girlfriend since they'd known each other since childhood. She didn't want money to be a problem so she "forgave" the debt. MoneyBags even shared the debt story with her dear friend. Moneybags wanted her to know why she totally ignored Dr. DegreedNot the night before, and she also wanted her to hear about the situation from her, not from HotPants and her crew.

MoneyBags caught wind of the gossip that HotPants was volunteering to share while popping crab legs at her grave table, you know, like a Red Table except conversations go to this table to die, to destroy individuals characters and create discord among the sistering. HotPants' table was a hot mess, full of crab juice and dipping sauce.

When MoneyBags destroyed all of the lies told by HotPants, Dr. DegreedNot's girlfriend understood and encouraged MoneyBags to go after her money. "He owes it, make him pay it," she would say.

MoneyBags knew she'd never see those dollars ever again so she didn't sweat it, she counted her loss and moved on but she was firm about her decision to never be social with Dr. DegreedNot, ever again. She felt he was the lowest of all lows because he borrowed money from a single mother knowing she needed it back. Dr. DegreedNot vowed to pay her back the very next day. The doctor claimed he left his wallet at home and was going to pay a bill. MoneyBags understood his dilemma and offered to help him out. She felt she could trust him since he'd been sniffing around her for a few weeks and bringing her lunch everyday. He would also sponsor pizza and movie nights for her kids. He was driving real nice and lived in one of the most expensive gated communities. *"Surley, he'll pay me back."* She thought to herself.

To her surprise, she had to ask for her money after the third day, unlike Jesus being raised from the dead, MoneyBags' account wouldn't recover the money she'd so freely shared with Dr DegreedNot. MoneyBags told the doctor, " Don't call me until you're man enough to pay me back." It would be years not seeing these dollars

Over the years, she'd see him out and clown him about her money.

This one particular time the doctor had enough of her calling him out. He responded,, "You still begging for that lil change?"

One thing about MoneyBags was she was kind, smart and important but if you hit that switch, she'd be mean, loud and aggressive.

Well, she was mean, loud and aggressive after saying that smart ass remark.

Her soul screamed: THIS NIGGA IS GONNA WISH HE PAID ME BACK! I ain't ask his slope head ass to pursue me. I'm always minding my business and here comes some needy ass nigga, always interrupting a woman during her evolution. Dis raggedy ass nigga just tried it.

[The "it" being MoneyBags last nerve.]

I don't know what's so attractive about a woman that's minding her own and doing her grown woman thing that grabs the attention of some tired, lying, insecure, my intentions ain't good for, bitch ass, punk ass, broke ass nigga." Her soul digressed.

The money was never paid. And MoneyBags was good with her loss. When Dr. DegreedNot started dating Moneybags's friend, she pulled back but, when you have messy crab eaters all up in your business, they pour fuel on dead fires. HotPants was messy but she masked it as care. She made it her mission to inform Dr. DegreedNot's new girl about his "old fling" MoneyBags.

MoneyBags was clueless She would get wind of the brew in the air and be the only one sipping tea at the end though. When

MoneyBags heard about her old business being aired by some old airbags, she took it upon herself to have a heart to heart with "the new girl."

It was squashed and like I shared earlier, the new girl was cool with MoneyBags and it could've stayed there.

When HotPants got wind that her dirt throwing conversation was blown away, that MoneyBags had a heart to heart with the doctor's girlfriend and their friendship remained intact, HotPants's messy radar went into overdrive. She didn't want peace to be a factor, she needed discord, something to gossip about at her grave table while popping crabs.

This brings us back to the Mother's Day Invitation:

"No, Dr. DegreedNot and his girl won't be here."

A lie ain't nothing for a miserable ass to tell. About an hour into the fish fry, Dr. DegreedNot and his girl showed up. MoneyBags was hot! She was ready to turn tables over! She looked at HotPants. *This lying BEEP*' MoneyBags would say in her inner soul. It wasn't a scream, just a final observation, confirming the seal to the end of a friendship. MoneyBags knew it was time to be done with HotPants.

It wasn't rocket science that this was all planned.

HotPants would be in Moneybags's ear all that night before. "Honey, he must be reminiscing about when he had you, look at how he's just staring at you, girl, he wants you."

MoneyBags just laughed and dropped it low to the music

because she knew HotPants was trying to get in her business, and she was dying to know if Dr. DegreedNot and MoneyBags ever rolled in them sheets. HotPants thought she knew what was up, and she wanted to hear it. Dr. DegreedNot lied to his girlfriend and said that MoneyBags was a "hater" because he chose her, the victim, and MoneyBags really wanted to be with him. HotPants shared that tea with MoneyBags.

MoneyBags was trying to figure out where HotPants was going with all of this. HotPants knew that MoneyBags didn't care for Dr. DegreedNot due to the money issue. "I want my money,'....." her soul continued to scream.

Back to the Mothers Day:

Dr DegreedNot and his victim, his girlfriend, arrive at HotPants house, Dr DegreedNot comes in hugging all the women and saying, "Happy Mothers Day." He waits to hug MoneyBag last. He's so sure of himself.

He goes in for the hug… "Happy Mothers Day, MoneyBags" he says.

She says, "Thank you."

Her SOUL SCREAMS: I know this nigga didn't just hug me. He touched me! Nigga, where is my money? MoneyBags plays it off. She holds her peace. Although it would sit on her chest like hot ashes. She knew she needed to do something to get her final point across.

MoneyBags would make sure this would be the last time this

crew would try her. If it wasn't one thing, it would be something else. MoneyBags knew that she needed to make a loud splash so this group would finally hear her.

MoneyBags remained kind and calm which left everyone in a state of confusion as they were sure she'd tear the place up. HotPants knew her friend, and she knew it wasn't over. She even gave her a "peace offering", trying to undo what she knew couldn't be overlooked by MoneyBags.

Two days had passed and MoneyBags went to Facebook live.

MoneyBags had started her own crusade for her very old debt. She knew she'd make enemies but she didn't care. She knew they were enemies all along so Moneybags would lose nothing.

The lives were freeing, liberating and hilarious. People would tune in, wanting to know who owed her…

HotPants would even join in. See, that was her character. She would throw rocks verbally and hide hands. She was getting a kick out of it all until MoneyBags turned her Facebook live in on her.

Shit just got real.

MoneyBags knew it was never about the money. She knew to remove herself from any activities HotPants would have because Dr. DegreedNot and his girl would be present. She knew to keep her calm and bow out gracefully. She really tried to allow this thing to die but HotPants just couldn't keep herself out of grown womenbusiness. HotPants stirred MoneyBags's pot one last time and those lil HotPants got burned. This would be one of MoneyBags most heartfelt Facebook lives ever. It was her eulogy to a friendship that ended years before it came down to this final verbal shootout. MoneyBags knew to end it this way. HotPants wasn't receiving MoneyBags' indirect direct facebook messages. She would secretly clown Dr. DegreedNot and she couldn't wait to tune in and listen to the next live show until she heard MoneyBags's decree, "Some people will never be true friends. You can't continue to ignore the person they really are, especially when they're comfortable inviting your enemy to sit with you at the same table to break bread."

MoneyBags accepted the truth about HotPants, the fact she never knew how to be a friend.

I know what you're thinking.

Did MoneyBags ever get her money?

Nope.

Would she run into Dr. DegreedNot again?

Yep, and he tried her again after all of the facebook live shade MoneyBags gave him.

Quick story:

Dr. DegreedNot tried to punk MoneyBags at this popular spot. He'd come over to the corner where MoneyBags was standing and stare her down while sipping on his drink and whispering something about MoneyBags in one of his partners ear. HotPants probably put him up to it since she and her crew were present.

Moneybags was a few drinks in and feeling her superpowers. She walks straight up to Dr. DegreedNot and with all the boldness of her soul she yells in his ear, "Where's my money, bitch?"

Her soul's scream was heard over the music. The crowd turned, the coward was shamed and walked away. He started crying to his lil girlfriend, HotPants and the crew.

See, sometimes your screams must be heard by those that come to silence you.

That's the lesson.

Free your soul and watch what follows.

Soul Lesson

Free your soul and watch what follows.

10

Sherules

A Lesson On Who Actually Rules The World

The Universe will allow you to peek into your soul and discover your divine self. Once you've experienced this introduction of who you really are, what you really want and why you've never been able to commit yourself to what is familiar to your flesh but unrecognizable to your soul, that's when you question all of your choices and all of the decisions you've made. You question everything because for the first time in your existence, you can actually recognize love. You learn that love rules the world.

She met her flame, her twin flame, the one her soul craved. She was currently in a "whatever this is" relationship with this person named Strings. She was dealing with ending her relationship with Strings, she knew it was time to move on. Her relationship with Strings was over, they met during a dry season in both of their lives. They identified it as a divine connection because it was made in the flesh. It wasn't divine though. It was very well camouflaged as something ordained by the powers that be. Maybe it was the powers that be disguising itself as love. That season that disguised itself as love would hold SheRules captive for years. Strings was clueless about how SheRules actually felt. She was good at denying herself and feeding others what she needed, unconditional nutritional love. Strings was comfortable with thinking that SheRules would always be there. And why not? It's been years and she's not demanding more.

There was a pattern with Strings behavior when it was time to be around SheRules and she took notice of it. He would make up excuses, not reply to her texts, ghost her, etc. She knew it was time for her to move on. She played fair. She'd played his game long enough. It was obvious he was very much into SheRules although he pretended not to be. After all, they were just "dating. They never made a verbal commitment, she'd stir up conversations about commitment and marriage and children, as she wanted children. She needed to know why she was so committed to this man, his ways and not to her own needs, her desires, her soul cries.

Strings wouldn't take her cries for more concerning their dating situation, more seriously. He'd do his thing and she'd continue to reach out until she couldn't reach out anymore. She wouldn't be strung along any longer. She knew she deserved to be someone's whole, as she was complete, and she needed her soul flame.

SheRules decided to shake all she was feeling and she talked herself out of breaking up with Strings. His birthday was coming up and SheRules wanted to share and celebrate. But he ignored SheRules birthday plans for him and created the argument that people create when they don't want to be bothered with you. SheRules saved him the trouble and told him to save his energy and do him. After all, it was his birthday and he could be an ass if he wanted to. He didn't realize he was the one being played by everyone he thought had his back. His extra attachments and those he thought loved him enough to at least get together and celebrate him. Strings would be wrong, and very disappointed.

Strings was left to celebrate alone and started reaching out to SheRules. She intentionally made herself unavailable. Strings needed to taste his own medicine and SheRules gave him a good dose. SheRules had no idea she was about to encounter the one that would make her forget about Strings.

Instead of being upset and ignoring Strings, SheRules called up her girls and they hit the clubs. They danced, laughed and dropped it hot and low.

"May I have this dance?" SheRules would hear.

She smiled and accepted the invitation.

He was dark and smooth. He was what she called BlackGold. He was in town for a short while but long enough to keep SheRules occupied and think…Strings who?

This would be just what SheRules needed.

Her soul screamed: IT'S LIKE HE'S KNOWN ME FOREVER. HE FEELS SO FAMILIAR. HIS SMELL, I'VE KNOWN IT BEFORE.

The music changes and she steps back to look at him, to make sure she's not going crazy. She wanted to see if she recognized his face from her past. Nope, this was a stranger to her natural eyes but her soul knew better. They'd keep company for the rest of the evening and danced as much as possible. SheRules wanted this moment to last. She desired not to return to the lonely memory of Strings.

The evening was coming to an end, this smooth dark and inviting man had asked SheRules for her number.

"Hand me your phone," she said.

She called her phone using his cell then logged his number in. She made sure to delete her number out of his phone once the call came through on her end.

"What did you do that for, how will I contact you? Why did you delete your number?" he asked.

She asked him his name.

"DarkMelanin," he replied.

She assigned DarkMelanin to the new number now locked in her phone.

The day after SheRules met her twin flame, she closed her chapters with Strings. He was not having it. He went out of his way to change SheRules mind about ending their "whatever this is" relationship. He'd remind her how good they were together and ask why throw away the years they've known each other. To him, what they had was good because it was convenient and it didn't demand anything from him. He could conveniently make himself available to her when he wanted to.

SheRules was done. Strings made it easy for her to give her attention to another man, her soul made it pleasing, her soul recognized DarkMelanin's soul. She wasted no time moving on.

DarkMelanin waited on SheRules to call, she made it worth his wait. She called, he didn't answer, he didn't recognize the number since she deleted her contact information. She sent a text: Hi, this is the young lady you danced with the other night, SheRules, give me a call when you're available.

Shortly after, her phone rang.

Her soul heard a sound that was so familiar, DarkMelanin's voice. Her flesh goosebumped.

Her soul smiled, and SheRules didn't understand what was going on because it was so natural and comforting and it is refreshing.

Strings made sure to make his presence known, he was determined not to be replaced. Not only did he want her back, he wanted marriage. He was desperate for the win.

DarkMelanin came in with his flame, burning up any memory, thought or feeling SheRules had remaining concerning Strings. DarkMelanin knew what he wanted and he went for it. He was up for the challenge but he knew Strings wasn't giving up SheRules that easily. "You're a good woman. He knows the loss and he's not letting you go," he expressed.

She wasn't worried about what Strings was up to, it was entertaining to her how Strings had all of this free time all of a sudden. It angered her, she'd given Strings her everything. When they were dating she gave him every opportunity to be to her what she now desired DarkMelanin to be, Her soulmate.

Everything was moving so fast and easy with SheRules and her new connection, Strings assumed DarkMelanin had been in

SheRules' life for a long time, as long as he was.

The feeling she'd get around DarkMelanin was new to her flesh but old in soul years. That was the vibe, the energy, and the connection she'd been longing for.

Strings was devastated, he wanted to know, "What is it about this dude?" He would pop up on their date nights and say it was a coincidence. SheRules knew better. He became obsessed with winning her back, not because he loved her or needed what she offered as a woman, but because he wanted to win. Nothing more, nothing less, he simply didn't want to feel like he'd lost something. DarkMelanin wasn't moved by all of the attention Strings was giving SheRules and their relationship. She was overjoyed to give all of herself and her attention to someone worthy of what she offered. She was a renaissance woman and she needed shoulders broad enough to carry all that she was. DarkMelanin was that soul.

Strings had gotten used to SheRules waiting on him, accepting what he offered. SheRules was just as much at fault as Strings was because she allowed herself to be whatever he needed in their relationship. Some would even go as far to say she sold her soul for him. She silenced the screams so she could enjoy the company of Strings, whenever he offered. DarkMelanin knew exactly what it was and encouraged her to meet with Strings, to get it all out on the table so he could move on with his shenanigans.

The conversation:

Strings: What is it, we were good, I feel we still are, you're just going through something. How in da hell are you in a relationship so fast anyway? You been knew him, … you had to.

SheRules: I can't explain what you can't comprehend. I met him the night you wanted to celebrate your birthday with yo peeps. You are the one who left the door open wide enough for me to receive what the universe wanted to give me. And yes, I received it with open arms. The gift was packaged so well, it had to be God who gave him to me.

Strings: I get it now. I love you. Fuck those other people, All they want is what I offer, they ain't bringing to the table what you bring. I get it. Give me another chance.

SheRules gets emotional, she begins to cry, her soul is screaming, her soul recognizes the lies but her flesh is deceived.

Later that evening, SheRules met with DarkMelanin, she was honest with him about how she felt. She loved DarkMelanin, she knew he was her soul's flame but she knew Strings flesh. She knew Strings the longest. She'd invested so much time and given so much energy to the years- long relationship she had with Strings. SheRules would allow years invested with Strings to trump what her soul connected to. She'd spiritually connected to DarkMelanin. She disappointed her soul and gave in to her flesh. Strings won his game. SheRules allowed herself to take a backseat to her soul self once again.

Life isn't long, it's short, even if you live to see one hundred years, it's short. We recite vows with individuals knowing we hear our soul, spirit and intuition screaming, "DON'T DO IT!" It screams way before we reach the altar, the judge, or the notary. There's something about the flesh that feels like we have something to prove when it comes to relationships. It's like we can't walk away from what obviously is no longer for us. We waste so many years making ourselves and others miserable because of the years invested, the gifts given and received or the child or children involved. The pension and the insurance all play a factor in our misguided choices. We humans tend to connect to flesh and kill our gift to ourselves, our freedom of choice.

Intuition suffers because we are so stubborn, clingy, and deceived when it comes to living in our truth. Love isn't confused nor confusing. We tend to get involved with certain entanglements because we have committed ourselves to situations that were never meant to be.   What's done is done; burnt, severed, finito!

Those are the type of relationships where people are walking around ashy and gloomy because of the smoke surrounding it. Talk about the walking dead.

If you're in this place, do yourself a solid favor, get out, especially if you are being abused in any way. There is a song that decrees that girls rule the world. That's the world's problem. It seems that children are ruling the world treating relationships as Childs play. Frankie said it best, "Too many games that people play."

Strings played SheRules. She became a part of his karma not realizing that bitch doesn't play. They would both regret getting involved once again with each other. Their relationship would always be a battle because there was no soul to be found.

11

Comphermize

A Lesson In How To Train A Dog
Not To Call You A Bitch

"Did this nigga just call me a bitch?" CompHERmize would ask her friend, Slick.

He sure did Comp. Slick responded.

(They called CompHERmize Comp for short.)

HalfStack was upset with Comp calling him out on his male chauvinistic comment.

HalfStack eased out of the view of CompHERmize's guy friends and muttered bitch under his breath because he knew her friends wouldn't appreciate this type of disrespect toward her. The evening started out nice. It was game night so CompHERmize hosted a small gathering. As the guys were entertained by the game, Comp and her friend Slick were spilling the tea. HalfStack wanted to be in the women's presence, so he jumped into their conversation. *Who invited him to the party?* Comp thought to herself.

Comp was known for speaking her mind and HalfStack was known for being the center of attention. Halfstack was constantly inserting his opinion where it wasn't needed. He had always been the ass of all jackasses. CompHERmize couldn't stand HalfStack but she tolerated a lot of unnecessary conversations and debates because her guy friend and HalfStack were boys. More like partners in crime because Comp noticed a lot about HalfStack that disturbed her, and her guy friend was comfortable with being "this type of guy" friend.

We've heard the saying "birds of a feather flock together."

However, when Comp thinks about this saying, it's hard for her to relate it to the type of people hanging together. Comp considers birds to be more intelligent than men because birds are committed to their flock. Most men on the other hand, will flock anywhere and commit to anything, especially men like HalfStack.

It bothered her that her guy was cool with a lot of HalfStack's slick ass ways.

Anytime HalfStack and CompHERmize would be in the same space, they would clash, like titans.

HalfStack wasn't ashamed about insulting women in front of women. "All women are bitches," he was heard saying. "All of them!" Comp didn't take this well, she addressed the insult and said, "I ain't no bitch. Yo momma is a bitch!" *How in the hell are you comfortable with saying that* she thought. *Especially in front of grown ass women including your lady?*

That thing didn't sit well with Comp, not well at all.

"What kind of punk is this?" Comp would think to herself. She knew then that she had no desire to entertain or even be in the presence of HalfStack. But he came with the "flock" that Comp would find herself flying along with.

For the sake of her guy friend, she would learn to adapt to the hostile environment she would often find herself in. Comp was really feeling this guy and it seemed his values and views of women were different. Her guy was kinder and displayed a gentleman's character. He didn't seem to fit in with the likes of

HalfStack. CompHERmize knew better, she knew there was a reason individuals like HalfStack kept the company of gullible folks like her guy. Her guy just wanted everyone to get along. He was good at holding a death ear and a blind eye to things that needed to be addressed. He would tell Comp, "Just let it go, it's not that serious, maybe they didn't mean it that way." For the sake of her relationship, Comp continued to tolerate the likes of bad company like HalfStack. She'd put her best fake forward anytime she'd be in the presence of HalfStack.

Why can't my guy see that this guy is a fake? What is it about this punk that's so appealing that my guy would consider him to be a loyal friend, even a brother?. Why can't he see what I see? There was no good here. This dude was poisonous. He needed to wake up. This evil was corrupting his good.

Comp soul's cry gave her guy one hell of a benefit of a doubt. She was aware it was difficult for two to walk together if they didn't agree.

CompHERmize would continue to date her guy despite his loyalty to HalfStack."He really is a great guy," she would say to herself." It wasn't everyday that she had to deal with HalfStack. "Afterall I'm not dating the bitch of the flock, I'm dating his friend." Disclaimer:

Any man that will fix his mouth to say, "All women are bitches," is the biggest bitch of them all. Finally, the day would come that HalfStack would try his chance at addressing Comp by his favorite pet name for women, in her home with her guy friend present. He wasn't bold enough to say it aloud though. He was the bitch of his flock so he knew not to call CompHERmize one out loud. He had enough cowardly sense to hide his face from her guy. He lowered his tone just enough to bark the word bitch at her.

"Did that nigga just call me a bitch?" Shocked and disturbed, she asks her friend Slick if that's what she heard.

"Sure did,!" Slick replied.

It was obvious to Comp that HalfStack had this on his heart to say for a while, especially after she'd put him in his place about his comment. I guess he had to validate his sick reasoning and his insecure conclusion about all women. He figured he'd accomplished his mission, to title CompHERmize with his term for women.

. Come on, did you think that Comp would keep such a betrayal of trust from her guy?

Of course, she told her guy. He was "shocked" and assured Comp that he'd handle it. He showed himself a man of his word and had the conversation with HalfStack. Her guy confronted HalfStack and made him apologize

The apology was half ass, just like the individual that was delivering it. It appears that you misunderstood the term I used the other night.," He said.

Comp walked away laughing sarcastically because he was such

a big joke to her that he would keep insulting her with an apology.

Knowing he was wrong and insincere he attempted the apology again.

"I apologize for calling you a bitch, I meant no harm," he would bring himself to choke up and say.

CompHERmize accepted the apology and accepted the fact she would have to compromise her dignity and entertain the likes of HalfStack if she desired to continue the relationship she had with her guy. Her soul wasn't pleased with her decision. ,She felt disturbed every time she'd be in HalfStacks's presence.

She still questioned the friendship between the two men because, although HalfStack apologized, Comp knew he didn't mean it. Nothing changed except that he'd never call CompHERmize bitch to her face again. She's certain he's still calling her that and so much more, behind her back, that's what bitches do.

When you want old things to pass away you must allow your thoughts to become new. Your actions are exposed thoughts. Pay close attention to them and you'll see just what they think about you. Pay attention to yourself and watch your inner thoughts reveal itself. Those are the thoughts you should place all your energy and focus on. It's not selfish to focus on yourself. We're taught, "It's not what they call you, it's what you respond to." Unlearn that shit! What they call you is what they are labeling you. Stop answering to their disrespect. Teach them your name the first time they "mispronounce" it!

12

Caddyknife

A Lesson on Identifying Whose Not The Sharpest Knife In The Kitchen

I told you all we'd get back to BakedBean.

Where should this fun and adventurous story begin?

Caddyknife loved herself a tall, dark and handsome (in his own rights) man. BakedBean was just that and Caddyknife didn't mind helping herself to what she wanted.

Caddyknife was a fancy and free-spirited individual and wasn't about to let the men have all the fun. She didn't fall for the miseducation of women, you know, wait on the man to approach you, date one man at a time, stay in the relationship regardless of his roaming, and keep giving him chances. It doesn't look good for a woman to have another relationship right after she's done with her previous one, so take your time. Make sure to have as many kids as you like, just make sure you only have one father for them. "Why are we following all of these crazy "men rule the world" stipulations society has placed on women being referred to as the mothers of earth and life givers. Who gave these dick swinging men all the power? Hell, if it wasn't for a woman, they wouldn't be here to have a say in what a woman sows into." Caddyknife thinks to herself when given advice not solicited from grown people. Generally speaking, of all the rules men make for women they don't practice themselves. Talk about double standards.

And let's not mention marriage. Scratch that, we're gonna mention it just for entertainment.

Caddyknife knew marriage wasn't for her. No one she dated

was found worthy enough for her to even want to commit her life to. Not even BakedBean. Let him tell her he was ready for marriage. Caddyknife issued a warning to BakedBean when she said, "Trust me, you aren't ready for marriage, especially with me. You may want to do some homework before you talk about marrying me."

He proposed anyway.

She gave him a kind no, and helped him to recall why. He swore to her he'd changed. He even began to show the outer signs of change. Eventually, Caddyknife gave him a yes, a trial yes.

She knew accepting his hands in marriage was a huge mistake. Caddyknife had just signed up for the ride of her life. Bean was a whore, a strong and solid, "I don't give a rat's ass" whore. But he was also a provider and hustler and Caddy needed that in her life. She needed the financial break. She saved her money and spent his. Signing up for this whore academy came with a price. It's called dropping your morals.

Caddy wasn't clueless nor desperate. She just needed a break. She needed someone to provide for her. Who better than the one who kept insisting? Bean challenged every area and nerve of Caddy's life. The secrets started pouring out and Caddy couldn't keep up. She became the ultimate spy, the heavyweight champ and superwoman all in this whirlwind of a relationship.

BakedBean started out as the daddy of six, and Caddyknife

was cool with that, he was a great dad, and the children, so respectful and loving. They'd pick the kids up on the weekends from four different houses. Yes, he had four different baby momma's. BakedBean's relationship with his children's mothers was a smooth sailing one. They respected their roles as parents, nothing more and nothing less.

Caddy loved how they all got along and they welcomed them in as well. They trusted her to pick up the children when Bean wasn't able to.

A few months passed and the engagement was developing beautifully. Beautifully until Caddyknife found out about another child. A child Bean wasn't "denying" but who he'd definitely kept a secret from Caddy.

Caddyknife's cousin caught wind of her engagement to BakedBean. Her cousin knew Bean very well. The child was her cousin's godchild. Caddy was caught off guard and Bean was shocked because he had no idea that his son's godmother was kin to his soon to be his wife. BakedBean had some explaining to do. He'd deny everything Caddy's cousin shared until he couldn't deny it anymore. A picture was worth a thousand DNA truths. He was, without question, that kid's father. The kid looked so much like BakedBean that it was like he was looking at a reflection of his younger self.

He wanted to keep this child a secret because he was still serving his child's mom. He was personally delivering the support she needed, sexual support.

Of course he denied it. Even in the same space at a jazz fest, he ignored his child's mother. She pulled a seat up to the dance floor and watched BakedBean fake being the committed, soon to be husband.

Caddyknife was clueless, she had no idea who the woman was until she noticed her cousin having a deep conversation with the woman in question. … Caddy put two and two together.

BakedBean children's status multiplied after that encounter. He decided to come clean with how many times he shared his ejaculations without a rubber on. BakedBean had fathered thirteen children that he knew of. Most of them didn't know about each other. Of the thirteen children, only six of them were acquainted with each other. This was because their mommas wouldn't take no mess.

His twin sister said it best: if it comes with a hole, he's guaranteed to stick his pole in it.

I told y'all BakedBean's story was a book, not a chapter. As you'd probably guessed, Caddyknife's soul wouldn't let her rest. Her soul would scream: GIRL, NOW YOU KNOW, WE AIN'T SIGN UP TO BE NOBODY'S QUEEN SAVE A HOE. IF YOU DON'T PACK OUR SHIT AND GET US UP OUT OF THIS CIRCUS. WE DON'T EVEN NEED TO HEAR FROM INTUITION. YOU CAN'T DO NOTHING WITH THIS BUT GIVE IT A PEACE OUT.

She ignores her soul cry, and *he's good for her pockets*, she thinks to herself. *My bank account is growing because I haven't paid a bill in months.* she added to the thought. *Thank God I requested an AIDS test.* BakedBean wasn't known for playing the field, he was known for leaving seeds. He was a sperm donor, just not the kind that goes into the sperm bank.

BakedBean was a whirlwind of a ride, Caddyknife would do her best to hold on. Caddyknife wanted Bean to work on getting his family reunion together. She made him realize that it was his own family reunion and suggested he get all of his children together. They needed to know their siblings. They needed to know why there were so many people in their town that looked like them.

Caddyknife decided to help BakedBean with this assignment. She would help him reach out to his children and share the news about the siblings they knew nothing about. It was working and Caddyknife began to see herself as the ultimate bonus mom. Afterall, she loved kids.

Unbeknownst to Bean, Caddyknife held out on moving forward with the wedding plans. She was still relating with him but no longer ignored her soul. Her intuition decided not to bail out on her. Soul and intuition knew Caddyknife needed them.

Once Caddyknife helped BakedBean smooth out his spreading of his seeds, once she observed how well he handled being the father of thirteen, she saw BakedBean in a different light. She started developing feelings for BakedBean beyond his providing pockets.

Her soul and intuition pricked her , as she could feel them whooping her ass in her gut. She could hear them saying, "You big dummy," in their Fred Sanford voices. She couldn't ignore them completely. They refused to bail on her. Soul and intuition knew Caddyknife would need them, and she was gonna need them soon.

Caddyknife would soon find out about BakedBean slipping his penis into several of her "girlfriends too."

The "girlfriends" actually started sharing their sexual escapade with BakedBean by telling Caddyknife she needed to watch her back with certain friends when it came down to her BakedBean.

"I heard that BakedBean and ole girl be fucking behind yo back.'

"Girl, you better watch that one, you see how comfortable he is with her, he's practically fucking her right in yo face…"

"Girl, you trust him with her? They mighty close, that's real comfortable."

Caddyknife was well seasoned in girl chat so she knew to watch the ones bringing the bones. Caddy needed eyes in the back, front and both sides of her head to keep up with all of her horny, hoe ass "girlfriends." She already knew BakedBean was down. Hell, it ain't like he adopted those thirteen children.

Caddyknife questioned it all, her girls were hot because Caddy went directly to the sources, not to the gossipers. Remember that cousin, his child's godmother? Yeah, Caddy recruited her cousin and they investigated the dirt. Needless to say, the gossip was true, BakedBean hadn't retired slinging dick for a living. He was providing the village and the "girlfriends" with dick meat.

Caddyknife was provided with her way out of the relationship. Her soul screamed:

DON'T PLOT, DO NOT SEEK REVENGE, JUST LEAVE. PACK YOUR GRIP AND GO.

She'd listen, make plans to leave, but she wanted her revenge. She wanted to retaliate on him and the slutty girlfriends but she also wanted to use him for one last payday.

She needed to catch him though. She wasn't able to get solid evidence of BakedBean's betrayal. She knew the sex stories were true but she couldn't get him to own up to what her girlfriends had spilled. What person would? What man would?

Fate and the universe would gift her with the perfect situation. And it was on a girl's night out with her truest friends. Caddyknife was hanging out with one of her most trusted sister friends, Kad. Kad didn't play when it came down to protecting her friend Caddy who was more like a sister to her. They were always there and down for whatever. On their night out, BakedBean kept calling and checking on them. It was out of the norm, he never called her on her girls night out. Caddy paid it no mind, she knew he was trying to "play good and concern" because of the sexual investigation Caddy had going on with him. She brushed it off as nervous and scared. Several calls later, Caddy and Kad knew something just wasn't right.

Caddyknife wanted to check it out for herself. She knew he was at his hangout spot. Kad pleaded for Caddy to go home, Kad knew despite her warning that she would do a drive by to see if Bean's car was in his favorite parking space. It was. Kad called Caddy to make sure she made it home safe, Caddy confessed and shared her location. "I'm hiding in the bushes to see who he's trying to spend this evening with," Caddy said. "I know he's trying to slip and get his slick on tonight, he called too many times."

"Girl, Please go home!" Kad begged.

"Ok, love you girl. Good night," Caddy replied.

Caddy didn't leave. She continued to hide in the bushes.

Just as she suspected, BakedBean was trying to get his freak on. Caddy watched as he walked out of this hole in the wall spot with two women, one on each arm. She watched him walk them to the car, and watched him purchase a pint of liquor and three plates from the food truck. She watched him walk casually to the car that the two women piled in. To his surprise, he had no idea that Caddyknife could fly, that she had wings. He placed one leg into the backseat of their car and sat on Caddyknife's lap. "Hey, you sitting on our food," the women screamed.

Caddy looked up at Bean and calmly asked, "Where we

going?"

She shares with the women, "I'm the future wife," and she flashes her ring that she picked out. The ring would be her last paycheck from Bean. Bean walked off, and Caddy walked behind him, doing her best to keep her calm, but she failed. She would end up jumping on Bean in the parking lot. Caddy felt her feet leave the ground, it would be the police jacking her up and throwing her on the hood of his car. The officer whispers in Caddy's ear, "I can't let you whoop that nigga ass in front of me, take it off the lot." Caddyknife understood the assignment, not in front of the cop.

BakedBean walked to get in his car, Caddy was still in her Super Woman Power strength. She got in her car and rammed it into Bean's, the officer and the entire hole in the wall parking lot watched the show. BakedBean walked away. He'd never been in a situation like this before. He should've known. BakedBean told Caddy that Peaches was his cousin from that last situation and they were giving her a ride home. This girl named Peaches!

Caddy responded, "Oh, that's what we're calling it now, cousin?"." She proceeded to whip his ass after Peaches went off on him. Caddy stood there and laughed. I'm sure his intuition warned him, "We better not fuck over this one. she's a thinker."

That ran good ole itty bitty Peaches off and apparently he didn't listen to his intuition.

Back to the night in question...

Caddyknife left her mark and a final message on the inside of BakedBeans car. Retrieving a blade she kept in her inner cheek, she sliced his luxury car seats up. She was so far removed from what she was doing, she didn't notice the blood flowing from the cuts from her fingers.

Caddyknife was pleased with her revenge although she was in pain from the razor cuts.

BakedBean knew it was over. He knew he had better move on and not reach out to Caddy. He would lick his emotional wounds and ask for his engagement ring back. And his toolbox. Wanna know what happened to the engagement ring? It paid a few bills and a few months on the rent. Caddy told him what pawnshop he could go to. He finally realized Caddyknife was never to be played with ever again.

I'm sure you are laughing at the relationship events that took place with this dysfunctional couple. I'm sure we have all played the fool. There are no exceptions to the fools rule. We recognize it as love. When we've never been introduced to love, we assume love hurts and deceives us. Love is such a victim to our definition of what we've made it to be and what we allow it to become when we refuse to move on. Lust is such a manipulator. It creates so many ways to disguise itself as love when love never entered the relationship. I'm not saying it's difficult to develop love with a character like BakedBean; anything is possible. You just have to give yourself a lot of credit when the skeletons in the closet start knocking you over your head. We are known for saying that people can be a "fool for love." When in actuality, fools should never taint the true meaning of love. Be true to your mission, your purpose, your reason why you involve yourself in matters of the heart. Stop fooling people with manipulation. When you know you have that one way about you, own your truth.

At least you're giving the person the option to choose whether or not they're willing to be your fool for "your definition of love' Instead of becoming an unaware victim of your foolishness.

ABOUT THE AUTHOR

Charletta Green is a free spirited person.
She loves life.
She loves unity.
She loves her husband.
She loves her children.
She adores her grandbabies.
She loves her parents, siblings, nieces and nephews.
She loves her bonus families: godchildren, bestfriends, buddys,
sister friends and brothers
She's abundantly blessed
She's a manifesting, positive speaking, affirmation writing, high
vibrational lifting, nature loving being.
She's been writing Screams of Your Soul since she was forty
nine years old.
She's glad to see it's finally done.
She enjoyed writing her first of many published books.

www.ingramcontent.com/pod-product-compliance
Lightning Source LLC
Chambersburg PA
CBHW041325120726
48005CB00014B/2135